I0648289

Herodotus, Alfred John Church

**Stories of Croesus, Cyrus and Babylon**

From Herodotus

Herodotus, Alfred John Church

**Stories of Croesus, Cyrus and Babylon**
*From Herodotus*

ISBN/EAN: 9783337195038

Printed in Europe, USA, Canada, Australia, Japan

Cover: Foto ©Andreas Hilbeck / pixelio.de

More available books at **www.hansebooks.com**

ENGLISH CLASSIC SERIES.—No. 115 116.

STORIES OF

# CRŒSUS, CYRUS AND BABYLON

## FROM HERODOTUS.

BY THE
### REV. ALFRED J. CHURCH, M.A.,
*Professor of Latin at University College, London;*
AUTHOR OF "STORIES FROM HOMER."

*PREPARED FOR READING IN SCHOOLS.*

With Introduction, Notes, Map, and Pronouncing
Vocabulary of Proper Names.

NEW YORK:
MAYNARD, MERRILL & CO., PUBLISHERS.

# A COMPLETE COURSE IN THE STUDY OF ENGLISH.

*Spelling, Language, Grammar, Composition, Literature.*

REED'S WORD LESSONS—A COMPLETE SPELLER.
REED'S INTRODUCTORY LANGUAGE WORK.
REED & KELLOGG'S GRADED LESSONS IN ENGLISH.
REED & KELLOGG'S HIGHER LESSONS IN ENGLISH.
REED & KELLOGG'S ONE-BOOK COURSE IN ENGLISH.
KELLOGG'S TEXT-BOOK ON RHETORIC.
KELLOGG'S TEXT-BOOK ON ENGLISH LITERATURE.

In the preparation of this series the authors have had one object clearly in view—to so develop the study of the English language as to present a complete, progressive course, from the Spelling-Book to the study of English Literature. The troublesome contradictions which arise in using books arranged by different authors on these subjects, and which require much time for explanation in the school-room, will be avoided by the use of the above "Complete Course."

Teachers are earnestly invited to examine these books.

## EFFINGHAM MAYNARD & CO., PUBLISHERS,

771 Broadway, New York.

# INTRODUCTION.

ONE of the most encouraging signs of improvement in the work of the schools is the substitution of literature itself for the literary fragments of the old-time reading-books. The discovery is made, at last, that the only way to secure good tastes and good reading habits is to bring children intimately and systematically in contact with good literature in the school-room, and not merely in the higher grades, but in all grades. To the end that the reading exercise may be in itself a pleasure for the pupil and a contribution to his permanent culture, the "English Classic Series" is furnishing essays, poems, and stories in their entirety, complete masterpieces from the best authors of English and American literature.

Professor Church's charming "Stories" from the ancient classics have established their right to a place among English classics, and their special fitness for the reading of young pupils will be appreciated in every school where knowledge and culture have the preference above discipline and drill. Of his stories from Herodotus two are given without abridgment in this number, the story of Crœsus and the story of Cyrus, constituting about one half of the volume entitled "Stories of the East." "In these stories," says Professor Church, "I have kept as close to my original as I could, but I do not profess to have translated it."

In preparing the text for school use a few notes have been added, intended mainly to serve as inducements and aids to further reading. A good classical dictionary should be frequently consulted. No attempt has been made to distinguish myth and fiction from fact and history. It is wiser to let the young imagination freely recreate for itself the ancient world, and leave to time and future reading the work of correction and readjustment of ideas. It would not be well, for example, to spoil a good story by explaining away the myth about the ch ldhood of Cyrus by the aid of modern scholarship, or to insist upon the improbability of Herodotus' account of his death, in view of the contradictory statements of other writers.

The attention of pupils may be directed to Professor Church's manner of writing, so far at least as to distinguish his style from that of other modern writers, and to recognize the appropriateness of its quaint simplicity and antique flavor in describing subjects so remote in time and place.

Much additional interest and profit will be derived from standard volumes of Eastern travel and archæological research. Ragozin's "Story. of Assyria," "Story of Chaldea," and "Story of Media, Babylon, and Persia" (Story of the Nations Series) are especially valuable. Rawlinson's "Five Great Monarchies" may also be consulted, and the same author's Translation of Herodotus.

J. W. A.

# HERODOTUS.

HERODOTUS, the "Father of History," was born about the year 484 B.C., in Halicarnassus, a Greek city of Asia Minor. This city was under Persian rule, and thus for thirty or more years he was a Persian subject. He was early inclined to study, perhaps by the influence of an uncle, Panyasis, an epic poet of fame, and soon made himself familiar with all the masterpieces of Greek literature. But he loved travel and the knowledge of living men quite as well as reading and the knowledge of books. So for many years he traveled, visiting all parts of Asia Minor, Greece, and the neighboring islands. He made the long and perilous journey to the Persian capital Susa, and visited Babylon, Scythia, and Colchis. He went to Palestine, explored the antiquities of Tyre, and made a long sojourn in Egypt, everywhere noting carefully the manners and customs of the people, their legends, history, and arts, the products of the land, the cities and modes of government. And thus by study and travel he was prepared, when nearly forty years of age, to write his great "History."

It was his main purpose to write a history of the struggle between Greece and Persia; but while tracing the growth of these great nations he naturally set forth the history of many subject nations, as Lydia, Media, Assyria, Scythia, Thrace, and Egypt. When the book was written he began to recite it to the citizens of his native town, for such was the method by which a book was then "published." But the prophet was without honor in his own land, for his countrymen ridiculed his splendid work. Angered and disheartened, he turned his back upon them forever, and went to Athens.

It was at the time of the great Pericles and the fascinating Aspasia, the golden age of Athenian art and culture. Here his recitations won such approval that he was given the sum of ten talents (twelve thousand dollars) by decree of the people, and he was received as a friend and an equal by the most distinguished artists, philosophers, and poets—Phidias, Zeno, Sophocles, Euripides, Thucydides, and many more. From this point in his career little is known of him, except that he spent much time in rewriting and perfecting his history. He would doubtless have spent the rest of his life in Athens, but such were the laws that he could not easily become a citizen, and among the Greeks it was thought an unworthy thing to be without citizenship. Accordingly, in the year 444 B.C., he went with a Greek colony to the new city of Thurii, in Italy, where he probably died at about the age of sixty.

Of the character of Herodotus' narrative Professor Church says: "I should be sorry that readers who are not acquainted with the work of the 'Father of History' should carry away from this book the impression that he is nothing more than a credulous and gossiping teller of stories. That he was often deceived, and that he writes with a simplicity which is quite remote from our ways of thinking, is manifest; but those who know him best are aware that he was nevertheless a shrewd and painstaking observer, whose credit has been distinctly increased by the discoveries of modern times."

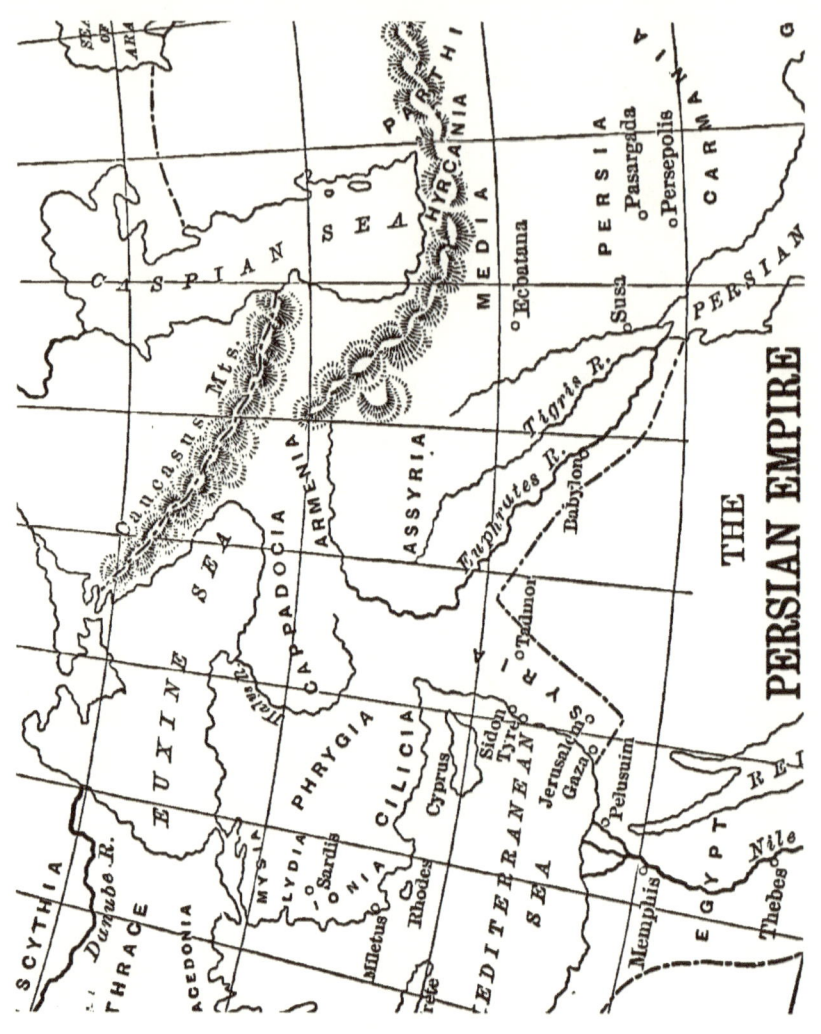

THE
PERSIAN EMPIRE

# CRŒSUS, CYRUS AND BABYLON

## from Herodotus.

---

## CHAPTER I.

### THE STORY OF KING CRŒSUS.

1. CRŒSUS, the son of Alyattes, began to reign over Lydia, being thirty and five years old. This Crœsus made war upon all the Greeks that dwelt in the western parts of Asia, seeking some occasion of quarrel with every city. And if he could find some great matter, he 5 used it gladly; but if not, a little thing would serve his turn.

2. Now the first of all the cities which he fought against was Ephesus; and when the Ephesians were besieged by him they offered their city as an offering to 10 the goddess Artemis, fastening a rope to the wall from

---

1. **Alyattes** (a-lī-at′teez): This king reigned over Lydia from 617 to 560 B.C. His tomb, north of Sardis, near Lake Gygæa, was a mound of earth, raised upon a foundation of great stones, nearly a mile in circumference. In recent years a room was found in the center of the mound, lined with polished white marble. But it had long been empty, having been plundered, probably, for the many precious things it contained. Sardis, his capital, was a splendid city, and through its market-place flowed the river Pactolus with its golden sands. Its site is now marked by the little village of *Sart*.

11. **Artemis** (ar′te-mis): One of the great divinities of the Greeks, called by the Romans Diana (di-a′na). She was the twin-sister of Apollo, and the protectress of the young, the flocks, and the chase. She was armed with a bow, quiver, and arrows. As her brother Apollo was god of the sun, so she

her temple. (The space between the temple and the wall was seven furlongs.) All the cities of the Greeks that are on the mainland did Crœsus subdue, so that they paid tribute to him. And when he had ended this 5 business, he purposed in his heart to build ships, and to make war on the Greeks that dwelt in the islands.

3. But when all things were now ready for the building of the ships, there came to Sardis a certain Greek, a man renowned for wisdom. Some say that this Greek 10 was Bias, the wise man of Priene, and some that he was Pittacus of Mitylene.

4. This Greek caused Crœsus to cease from his shipbuilding, for when the King would know whether he had any news from Greece, he said to him, " O King, 15 the islanders are buying ten thousand horses, that they may set riders upon them, and so march against thee and thy city of Sardis."

5. When Crœsus heard this he was glad, hoping that the man spake truth, and said, " Now may the Gods 20 put this into the hearts of the islanders, that they should make war with horses against the sons of the Lydians." Then the Greek answered and said, " O King, I see that thou prayest with all thy heart that thou mayest find the islanders coming against thee here on the mainland 25 with horses, and verily thou doest well. What then dost thou think that the islanders pray for now that

---

was also goddess of the moon; as such she was represented to be in love with the fair youth Endymion (en-dim'I-on), whom she kissed in his sleep. The Ephesian Artemis differed somewhat from this Greek goddess, being worshiped as the goddess of the all-nourishing powers of nature; hence her image in the great temple of Ephesus represented her with many breasts. Her splendid temple was regarded as one of the seven wonders of the world.

10. **Bias**: This Bias of Priene (pri-e'ne) in Ionia was accounted one of the seven wise men of Greece. **Pittacus** of Mitylene (mit-i-le'ne) was another of the "seven sages," celebrated both as a warrior and as a philosopher. Two famous maxims were ascribed to him, " Know the fittting moment," and " It is a misfortune to be eminent."

they know thee to be building ships ?   Surely that they
may find the Lydians coming against them on the sea,
that so they may take vengeance on thee for their
brethren on the mainland, whom thou hast brought into
slavery."                                                                                    5

6. This saying pleased King Crœsus mightily; and
because the Greek seemed to him to speak truly, he
ceased straightway from his ship-building, and made
alliance with the Greeks that dwelt in the islands.

7. Now after certain years, when all Asia that lieth 10
to the westward of the river Halys had been subdued
by Crœsus (only Lycia and Cilicia were not subdued),
and his kingdom flourished with great wealth and
honor, there came to Sardis all the wise men of the
Greeks, as many as there were in those days.   But the 15
greatest of all that came was Solon of Athens.

8. This Solon had made laws for the Athenians, for
they would have him make them, and afterward he
dwelt abroad for ten years.   And he said that he did this
that he might see foreign countries ; but in truth he 20
departed that he might not be compelled to change any
of the laws that he had made.   For the Athenians themselves could not change any, having bound themselves
with great oaths to Solon, that they would live for the
space of ten years under the laws which he had made 25
for them.

9. Solon therefore came to Sardis, and Crœsus enter-
tained him in his palace.   And on the third or fourth
day after his coming the King commanded his servants

---

16. **Solon :** Pupils will take pleasure in reading the account of this great
law-giver and his wise and patriotic work in Plutarch's Lives.  The consti-
tution which he gave to the Athenians, and the many excellent reforms
which he accomplished, are fully described in Grote's History of Greece,
Vol. III.

that they should show Solon all the royal treasures.   So the servants showed him all the things that the King possessed, a very great store of riches.

10. And when he had seen everything and considered
5 it, and a fitting time was come, the King said to him, " Man of Athens, I have heard much of thee in time past, of thy wisdom and of thy journeyings to and fro, for they say that thou wanderest over many lands, seeking for knowledge.   I have therefore a desire to ask of
10 thee one question: 'Whom thinkest thou to be the happiest of all the men that thou hast seen?'"

11. And this he said hoping that Solon would answer, " Thou, O King, art the happiest man that I have seen." But Solon flattered him not a whit, but spake the truth,
15 saying, "O King, the happiest man that I have seen was Tellus the Athenian."   Then Crœsus, marveling much at these words, said, "And why thinkest thou that Tellus the Athenian was the happiest of men?"

12. Then Solon answered, " Tellus saw his country in
20 great prosperity, and he had children born to him that were fair and noble, and to each of these also he saw children born, of whom there died not one.   Thus did all things prosper with him in life, as we count prosperity, and the end of his days also was great and
25 glorious; for when the Athenians fought with certain neighbors of theirs in Eleusis, he came to the help of his countrymen against their enemies, and put these to flight, and so died with great honor; and the whole people of the Athenians buried him in the same place
30 wherein he fell, and honored him greatly."

13. But when Solon had ended speaking to the King of Tellus, how happy he was, the King asked him again, " Whom, then, hast thou seen that was next in happiness

to this Tellus?" For he thought to himself, "Surely now he will give me the second place." Then Solon said, "I judge Cleobis and Biton to have been second in happiness to Tellus."

14. Cleobis and Biton were youths of the city of 5 Argos. They had a livelihood such as sufficed them; and their strength was greater than that of other men. For not only did they win prizes of strength, but also they did this thing that shall now be told.

15. The men of Argos held a feast to Heré, who hath 10 a great and famous temple in their city; and it must needs be that the mother of the two young men, being priestess of Heré, should be drawn in a wagon from the city to the temple; but the oxen that should have drawn the wagon were not yet come from the fields. 15

16. Then, as the time pressed and the matter was urgent, the young men harnessed themselves to the wagon and dragged it, and their mother the priestess sat upon it. And the space for which they dragged it was forty and five furlongs; and so they came to the 20 temple.

17. And when they had done this in the eyes of all the assembly, there befell them such a death that nothing could be more to be desired; the Gods, indeed, making it manifest that it is far better for a man to die 25 than to live. For indeed the thing fell out thus.

18. When all the people of Argos came about the

---

13. **Heré** (he're): The Greek name of Juno, who was the wife of Jupiter (Zeus), and therefore queen of heaven (Olympus). At her marriage all the gods honored her with presents, and Terra (the earth) gave her a tree with golden apples, which was guarded by the Hesperides (hes-per'i-deez) at the foot of Mt. Atlas. Because Paris decided that Venus was more beautiful than Juno, she hated the Trojans, and was on the side of the Greeks in the Trojan war. She was the goddess of marriage, and splendid festivals were held at her temple in Argos. She was depicted with bridal veil, diadem, and scepter, and a peacock at her side. See Classical Dictionary under *Juno, Hesperides,* and *Paris.*

woman and her sons, and the men praised the youths
for their great strength, and the women praised the
mother that she had borne such noble sons, the mother
in the joy of her heart stood before the image and
5 prayed that the goddess would give to her sons, even
Cleobis and Biton, that which the Gods judge it best
for a man to have.

19. And when the priestess had so prayed, and the
young men had offered sacrifice, and made merry with
10 their companions, they lay down to sleep in the temple,
and woke not again, but so ended their days. And the
men of Argos commanded the artificers that they
should make statues of the young men, and these they
offered to the god at Delphi.

15    20. But when Solon thus gave the second place of
happiness to these young men, King Crœsus was very
wroth, and said, "Man of Athens, thou countest my
happiness as nothing worth, not deeming me fit to be
compared even with common men."

20    21. Then Solon made answer, "O Crœsus, thou askest
me about mortal life to say whether it be happy or no,
but I know that the Gods are jealous and apt to bring
trouble upon men. I know also that if a man's years
be prolonged he shall see many things that he would
25 fain not see, aye, and suffer many things also.

22. "Now I reckon that the years of a man's life are
threescore and ten, and that in these years there are
twenty and five thousand days and two hundred. For
this is the number, if a man reckon not the intercalated
30 month. But if he reckon this, seeing that in threescore
and ten years are thirty and five such months, and the

---

27. **Threescore and ten**: "The days of our years are threescore years
and ten."—*Psalms*, xc. 10.

days of these months are one thousand and fifty, then the whole sum of the days of a man's life is twenty and six thousand two hundred and fifty.

23. "Now of these days, being so many, not one bringeth to a man things like to those which another hath 5 brought. Wherefore, O King, the whole life of man is full of chance. I see indeed that thou hast exceeding great wealth and art king of many men. But as to that which thou askest of me, I call thee not happy, till I shall know that thou hast ended thy days prosperously. 10

24. "For the man that hath exceeding great riches is in no wise happier than he that hath sufficient only for the day, unless good fortune also remain with him, and give him all things that are to be desired, even unto the end of his days. 15

25. "For many men that are wealthy beyond measure are nevertheless unhappy, and many that have neither poverty nor riches have yet great happiness, and he that is exceeding rich and unhappy withal, excelleth him that hath moderate possessions with happiness in two 20 things only, but the other excelleth in many things.

26. "For the first hath the more strength to satisfy the desires of his soul, and also to bear up against any misfortune that cometh upon him; but the second hath not this strength; and indeed he needeth it 25 not, for his good fortune keepeth such things far from him. Also he is whole in body, and of good health, neither doth misfortune trouble him, and he hath good children, and is fair to look upon.

27. "And if, over and above these things, he also end 30

3. Herodotus makes Solon count his months at 30 days each; but the Greek months were alternately of 29 and 30 days, and the years were alternately of 12 and 13 months, with the inserted or intercalary month omitted once in eight years. Thus Herodotus makes the amount much too large.

his life well, then I judge him to be the happy man whom thou seekest. But till he die, so long do I hold my judgment, and call him not happy indeed, but fortunate.

5    28. "It is impossible also that any man should comprehend in his life all things that be good. For even as a country sufficeth not for itself nor produceth all things, but hath certain things of its own and receiveth certain from others, and as that country which pro-
10 duceth the most is counted the best, even so is it with men, for no man's body sufficeth for all things, but hath one thing and lacketh another.

29. "Whosoever, O King, keepeth ever the greatest store of things, and so endeth his life in a seemly
15 fashion, this man deserveth in my judgment to be called happy. But we must needs regard the end of all things, how they shall turn out; for the Gods give to many men some earnest of happiness, but yet in the end overthrow them utterly."

20    30. These were the words of Solon. But they pleased not King Crœsus by any means. Therefore the King made no account of him, and dismissed him as being a foolish and ignorant person, seeing that he took no heed of the blessings that men have in their hands, bidding
25 them always have regard unto their end.

31. Now it came to pass after Solon had departed from Sardis that there came great wrath from the Gods upon King Crœsus, and this, doubtless, because he judged himself to be the happiest of all men.

30    32. And it happened in this wise. He saw a vision in his sleep, that told him of the trouble that should come upon him with respect to his son. For the King had two sons; but the one was afflicted of the Gods,

being dumb from his birth, but the other far surpassed his equals of age in all things. And the name of this son was Atys.

33. Now the vision that he saw in his sleep showed him that Atys should be smitten with a spear-point of iron, and so die. Therefore when he woke from his sleep and considered the matter, being much terrified by the dream, he sought how he might best keep his son from this peril.

34. First, then, he married him to a wife; and next, he suffered him not to go forth any more to battle, though he had been wont aforetime to be the captain of the host; and, besides all this, he took away all javelins and spears, and such like things that men are wont to use in battle, from the chambers of the men, and stored them elsewhere, lest perchance one of them should fall from its place where it hung upon the wall and give the youth a hurt.

35. Now it chanced that while the matter of the young man's marriage was in hand, there came to Sardis a certain stranger, upon whom there had come the great trouble of blood-guiltiness. The man was a Phrygian by birth, and of the royal house: and he came into the palace of Crœsus, after the custom of that country, and sought for one that should cleanse him from his guilt; and Crœsus cleansed him. (Now the manner of cleansing is the same, for the most part, among the Lydians as it is among the Greeks.)

---

25. According to the custom, the person seeking to be cleansed entered the house of a stranger, threw himself upon the hearth, stuck his sword into the ground, and covered his face with his hands. The master of the house then sacrificed a pig, and washed the hands of the guilty person in the blood. After the sacrifice had been properly performed the name of the fugitive was asked, and the circumstances of his crime. Such rites of purification formed an important part of the religious practices of the ancients. See Encyclopædia Britannica under *Lustration*.

36. And when the King had done for him according to all that was prescribed in the law, he would fain know who he was, and whence he had come. Wherefore, he asked him, saying, " My friend, who art thou? and from what city of Phrygia—for that thou art a Phrygian I know—art thou come, taking sanctury at my hearth? And what man or woman didst thou slay?"

37. And the man answered, " O King, I am the son of Gordias, the son of Midas, and my name is Adrastus, and I slew my own brother, not wittingly. For this cause am I come to thee, for my father drave me out from my home, and I am utterly bereft of all things."

38. To this King Crœsus made reply, " Thou art the son of friends, and to a friend art thou come. Verily as long as thou abidest here thou shalt lack for nothing that I can give thee. And as for thy trouble, it will be best for thee to bear it as easily as may be." So the man lived thenceforth in the King's palace.

39. Now about this time there was a mighty wild boar in Olympus, that is a mountain of Mysia. It had its den in the mountain, and going out thence did

---

10. **Gordias :** It was the chariot of this ancient king of Phrygia that Alexander found at Gordium. The yoke was fastened to the pole by a knot of bark, and an oracle had said that he who untied this knot should rule over all Asia. Alexander cut the " Gordian Knot " and thus applied the prophecy to himself.

10. **Midas** (mī'das): Midas was the king who so loved wealth that he prayed the god Bacchus to grant him the favor that all things which he touched might be turned to gold. But when even the food that he touched became gold, he implored the god to take back his favor. Thereupon Bacchus sent him to bathe in the river Pactolus, and thus he was saved, but ever after the sand of the river was filled with gold. Once, in a musical contest between Pan and Apollo, Midas decided in favor of Pan, and for his bad taste Apollo changed his ears to ass's ears. Midas concealed th..m under his Phrygian cap, but a servant discovered the secret, and being unable to keep it, yet afraid to reveal it, dug a hole in the earth and whispered into it, " King Midas has ass's ears ;" and he filled the hole again, but the reeds that grew there whispered the secret to the winds forever after. Read Hawthorne's delightful version of the story of Midas, "The Golden Touch," in the " Wonder Book."

much damage to the possessions of the Mysians ; and
the Mysians had often sought to slay him, but harmed
him not at all, but rather received harm themselves.

40. At the last they sent messengers to the King ;
who stood before him, and said, " O King, a mighty 5
monster of a wild boar hath his abode in our country
and destroyeth our possessions, and though we would
fain kill him we cannot.  Now therefore we pray thee
that thou wilt send thy son, and chosen youths with
him, and dogs for hunting, that they may go with us, 10
and that we may drive this great beast out of our land."

41. But when they made this request Crœsus remem-
bered the dream which he had dreamed, and said, " As
to my son, talk no more about him, for I will by no
means let him go, seeing that the youth is newly mar- 15
ried to a wife, and careth now for other things.  But
chosen youths of the Lydians shall go with you, and all
the hunting dogs that I have ; and I will bid them do
their utmost to help you, that ye may drive this wild
beast out of your land."   This was the King's answer; 20
and the Mysians were fain to be content with it.

42. But in the meanwhile the youth came in, for he
had heard what the Mysians demanded of his father;
and he spake to the King, saying, " O my father, I was
wont aforetime to win for myself great credit and honor 25
going forth to battle and to hunting.  But now thou
forbiddest me both the one and the other, not having
seen any cowardice in me or lack of spirit.  Tell me,
my father, what countenance can I show to my fellows
when I go to the market, or when I come from thence ? 30
What manner of man do I seem to be to my countrymen? and what manner of man to the wife that I have
newly married ?   What thinketh she of her husband ?

Let me therefore go to this hunting, or, if not, prove to me that it is better for me to live as I am living this day."

43. To this Crœsus made answer, "My son, I have
5 seen no cowardice or baseness or any such thing in thee ; but there appeared to me a vision in my sleep, and it stood over me and said that thy days should be few, for that thou shouldest die being smitten by a spear-point of iron.   For this reason I made this marriage for
10 thee, and send thee not forth on such occasions as I was wont to send thee on, keeping thee under guard, if so be that I may shield thee from thy fate at the least so long as I shall live.   For thou art now my only son, for of him whom the Gods have afflicted, making him
15 dumb, I take no count."

44. To this the young man made answer, "Thou hast good reason, my father, to keep guard over me, seeing that thou hast had such a dream concerning me; yet I will tell thee a thing that thou hast not understood nor
20 comprehended in the dream.   Thou sayest that the vision told thee that I should perish by a spear-point of iron.   Consider now, therefore, what hands hath a wild boar and what spear-point of iron, that thou shouldest fear for me ?   For if indeed the vision had said that I
25 should perish by a tooth, or by any other thing that is like to a tooth, then thou mightest well do what thou doest ; but seeing that it spake of a spear-point, not so. Now, therefore, that we have not to do battle with men, but with beasts, I pray thee that thou let me go."

30   45. Then said King Crœsus, "It is well said, my son ; as to the dream, thou hast persuaded me.   Therefore I have changed my purpose, and suffer thee to go to this hunting."   When he had said this, he sent for Adrastus

the Phrygian ; and when the man was come into his presence, he spake, saying, " Adrastus, I took thee when thou wast afflicted with a grievous trouble, though indeed with this I upbraid thee not, and I cleansed thee from thy guilt, and received thee into my palace, and 5 sustained thee without any cost of thine.

46. "Now, therefore, it is well that thou shouldest make me some return for all these benefits. I would make thee keeper of my son now that he goeth forth to this hunting, if it should chance that any robbers or 10 such folk should be found on the way to do him hurt. Moreover, it becometh thee, for thine own sake, to go on an errand from which thou mayest win renown; for thou art of a royal house and art besides valiant and strong." 15

47. To this Adrastus made answer, " O King, I had not indeed gone to this sport but for thy words. For he to whom such trouble hath come as hath come to me should not company with happy men ; nor indeed hath he the will to do it.   But now, as thou art earnest 20 in this matter, I must needs yield to thy request. Therefore I am ready to do as thou wilt ; be sure, therefore, that I will deliver thee thy son, whom thou biddest me keep, safe and unhurt, so far as his keeper may so do." 25

48. So the young men departed, and chosen youths with them, and dogs for hunting.  And when they were come to the mountain of Olympus they searched for the wild boar, and when they had found it, they stood in a circle about it, and threw their spears at it. 30

49. And so it fell out that this stranger, the same that had been cleansed from the guilt of manslaying, whose name was Adrastus, throwing his spear at the

wild boar and missing his aim, smote the son of Crœsus.
And the youth died of the wound, so that the vision of
the King was fulfilled, that he should die by a spear-
point.    And straightway there ran one to tell the thing
5 to Crœsus.    And when he had come to Sardis, he told
the King how they had fought with the wild boar, and
how his son had died.

50.  Crœsus was very grievously troubled by the death
of his son ; and this the more because he had been slain
10 by the man whom he had himself cleansed from the
guilt of blood.    And in his great grief he cried out very
vehemently against the Gods, and specially against
Zeus, the god of cleansing, seeing that he had cleansed
this stranger, and now suffered grievous wrong at his
15 hands.

51.  He reproached him also as the god of hospitality
and of friendship—of hospitality, because he had enter-
tained this man, and knew not that he was entertaining
the slayer of his own son ; and of friendship, because he
20 had sent him to be a keeper and friend to his son, yet
had found him to be an enemy and destroyer.

52.  And when he had done speaking there came
Lydians bearing the dead body of the young man, and
the slayer followed behind.    So soon, therefore, as the
25 man was come into the presence of the King, he gave
himself up, stretching forth his hands, and bidding
the King slay him on the dead body.    And he spake of
the dreadful deed that he had done before, and that
now he had added to it a worse thing, bringing de-

---

13. **Zeus** : Jupiter, the father of gods and men, and supreme ruler.  He
dwelt on Mount Olympus, whose summit, it was believed, reached up to
heaven.  He exercised special protecting care over public assemblies and
private households, and also the sacred oaths and obligations among men.
Thunder and lightning were his weapons, and the scepter and the eagle
were the symbols of his power.

struction on him that had cleansed him ; and he cried out that he was not fit to live.

53. But when Crœsus heard him speak, he pitied him, for all that he was in grievous trouble of his own, and spake to him, "I have had from thee, O my friend, 5 all the vengeance that I need, seeing that thou hast pronounced sentence of death against thyself. But indeed thou art not the cause of this trouble, save only that thou hast brought it to pass unwittingly; some god is the cause, the same that long since foretold to 10 me this very thing that hath now befallen me."

54. So Crœsus buried his son with all due rites. But Adrastus the son of Gordias the son of Midas, that had been the slayer of his own brother, and had now slain the son of him that had cleansed him, waited behind 15 till all men had left the sepulchre, and then slew himself upon it; for he knew that of all the men in the world he was the most unhappy.

———— •

# CHAPTER II.

CRŒSUS, WISHING TO MAKE WAR AGAINST THE PER-
SIANS, CONSULTETH THE ORACLES.

1. For the space of two years did King Crœsus sit sorrowing for his son. But in the third year his 20 thoughts were turned to other matters. For he heard that the kingdom of Astyages the son of Cyaxares had

---

22. The story of Astyages (as-ti'a-jeez), King of Media, and Cyrus, the son of Cambyses (kam-bi'seez), is given in Chap. V. Cyaxares (si-aks'a-reez) was the great general who conquered the Assyrians and destroyed Nineveh.

been overthrown by Cyrus the son of Cambyses, and
that the power of the Persians increased day by day.
For which reason it seemed good to him that he should
prevent this people, if by any means he could, before
5 they should become too mighty for him.

2. And so soon as he had conceived this purpose in his
heart, he made trial of all the oracles that are both in
Europe and in Asia, sending messengers to Delphi, and
to Abæ that belongeth to Phocis, and to Dodona.    Also
10 he sent to the oracles of Amphiaraüs, and of Trophonius, and of Branchidæ that is in Miletus.    These are
the oracles in the land of Greece of which he sent to
inquire, and in Libya he sent to the oracle of Hammon.

---

**4. Prevent:** This word is from two Latin words, *præ*, before, and *venire*,
to come; hence it means here to get the start of, to be beforehand with
this people, and so stop or restrain their growing power.

**7.** Read, if possible, the article " Oracle " in the Encyclopædia Britannica,
Vol. XVII.

**8. Delphi :** The oracle of Apollo at Delphi was the most celebrated
oracle of the Greeks.    In the center of the great temple was a small opening
in the ground from which an intoxicating vapor arose.    Over this stood a
tripod, on which the priestess Pythia (pith'ĭ-a) sat, when the oracle was to
be consulted.    The words that she uttered after inhaling the vapor were
carefully written down in verse by the attendant priests and given to the
persons who had come to consult the oracle.

**9. Abæ** (a'be): A town of Phocis, which possessed an ancient temple and
oracle of Apollo.

**9. Dodona** (do-do'na): The most ancient oracle in Greece, in Epirus.
The responses of the oracle were given from lofty oak trees, by means of
the wind rushing through the branches.

**10. Amphiaraus** (am-fĭ-a-ra'us): A great prophet and hero.    In the war
against Thebes he was about to be slain when Jupiter struck the earth with
a thunderbolt and it opened and swallowed up the hero, with his horses
and chariot.    On this spot was his oracle.    The inquirer who consulted this
oracle was obliged to abstain from wine for three days and from all food
for twenty-four hours, and to sleep in the temple on the skin of a ram
which he had sacrificed.

**10. Trophonius** (tro-fo'nĭ-us): An architect who with his brother Agamedes (ag-a-me'deez) built the temple at Delphi.    After death he was worshiped as a hero and had an oracle in a cave in Bœotia.    It was believed
that he who entered the cave saw such sights that he never smiled again.

**11. Branchidæ** (bran'ki-de): A place on the coast of Ionia, where were a
much esteemed oracle and temple of Apollo.    The ruins of the grand
temple still exist.    One traveler says of it: " The columns, yet entire, are so
exquisitely fine, the marble mass so vast and noble, that it is impossible,
perhaps, to conceive greater beauty and majesty of ruin."

**13. Hammon :** Ammon, or Jupiter Ammon, an Egyptian divinity, whose
celebrated oracle was in an oasis in the Lybian desert.    This oracle was visited by Alexander.

3. First he sent to make trial of all these whether they should be found to know the truth about a certain thing, purposing that if they should be so found he would send to them yet again and inquire whether he should take it in hand to make war against the Persians. 5

4. Now he had given commandment to the messengers whom he sent to make trial of the oracles, that they should reckon the days diligently from the day whereon they set out from Sardis, and that on the hundredth day they should inquire of the oracles, say- 10 ing, " What doth Crœsus the son of Alyattes, king of Lydia, chance to be doing this day ?" and that they should write down the words of the oracle and bring them back to him.

5. Now what the other oracles answered no man 15 knows; but at Delphi, so soon as the Lydians were come into the temple to inquire of the god, the Pythia, for so they call the priestess that uttereth the mind of the god, spake, saying—

"I know the number of the sand,                    20
    I know the measures of the sea ;
  The dumb man's speech I understand,
    Though naught he say, 'tis clear to me.
  I smell a savor new and sweet ;
    Strange is the feast the Lydians keep ;        25
  Mingled in brazen caldron meet
    The tortoise flesh and flesh of sheep ;
  Around the burning embers glow,
  With brass above and brass below."

6. These words the Lydians wrote down from the 30 mouth of the Pythia, and so departed, and went their way to Sardis. The other messengers also came, bringing with them the oracles that had been delivered to them. Then the King opened each and read the writ-

ing; and not one of them pleased him. But when he knew the answer that had been brought from Delphi, forthwith he prayed and received it with reverence, for he judged that there was no true oracle in the world 5 save that of Delphi only, seeing that it had discovered the very thing that he was doing.

7. For after that he had sent his messengers to the oracles, when the appointed day was come, he devised this device. He imagined something that could not, 10 he thought, by any means be discovered; for he chopped up together the flesh of a tortoise and the flesh of a lamb, and cooked them himself in a brazen caldron, upon which he had put a lid of brass.

8. This was the answer that came to Crœsus from 15 Delphi; but as to the oracle of Amphiaraüs, the answer that it made to the messengers when they had duly inquired of it no man knows, yet did Crœsus think that this also was a true oracle.

9. Here shall be told the story of Alcmæon of Athens, 20 to whom Crœsus sent bidding him come to Sardis, for that he had helped the King's messengers when they inquired of the god at Delphi, furthering their business with all diligence. And when Alcmæon was come, the King said to him that he should be permitted to 25 go into his treasury, and take therefrom for himself all the gold that he could carry on his body.

10. Then Alcmæon prepared himself for this business. First he clothed himself with a tunic, in which he made a great fold for a pocket; and next he got him 30 the widest and biggest boots that he could find, and so went into the treasury. And lighting on a heap of dust of gold he filled his boots with it as much as they would contain, even up to his knees; and also the fold

of his tunic he filled with gold; also into his hair he put so much of the dust as it would contain. Other gold he took into his mouth, and so made his way out of the treasury, but scarcely could he drag his boots after him; and indeed he seemed like to anything rather than to 5 a man, for his mouth was filled out and swollen beyond all a man's semblance.

11. And when Crœsus saw him he laughed, and gave him all that gold and as much more. This was the beginning of the wealth of the house of Alcmæon.   10

12. After this King Crœsus sought to propitiate the god that was in Delphi with many and great sacrifices. For first he sacrificed three thousand beasts of all such as it is lawful to offer to the Gods, and next he builded up a great pile of couches that were covered with gold 15 and silver, and of cups of gold, and of purple garments and tunics, and set fire to the pile, for he thought that by so doing he should make the god a friend to him.

13. And he gave commandment to the Lydians that they should sacrifice in like manner every one of them 20 such things as they had. And when this sacrifice was ended, he melted a great store of gold, and made bricks of it. Of these the bigger sort were six hand-breadths in length, and the smaller three hand-breadths, and all of them a hand-breadth in height.   25

14. There were one hundred and sixteen of these bricks in all, four of them being of pure gold, and weighing each one talent and half a talent, and the rest of gold that was mixed with alloy; these weighed two talents to the brick. Also he made the image of a lion 30 of pure gold, ten talents in weight. This lion, when

---

10. **House of Alcmæon :** This was a famous family of Athens, called after the founder *Alcmæonidæ* (alk-me-on'i-de).
31. The lion was the royal emblem of Lydia, and a lion's head was stamped on the Lydian coins.

the temple of Delphi was burnt, fell down from the bricks (for it had been set up on them); and now it lieth in the treasury of the Corinthians, and weigheth seven talents and half a talent.

5  15. When Crœsus had finished casting these bricks, he sent them to Delphi and other things with them; to wit, two very great mixing bowls, of gold the one, and of silver the other.  The bowl of gold lieth now in the treasury of the Corinthians, being in weight four talents 10 and half a talent and twelve ounces.  And the silver bowl lieth in the corner of the ante-chamber.  It holdeth six hundred firkins; and the Delphians mix wine in it at the feast of the Showing of the Images.

15  16. Also he sent four silver casks, that stand now in the treasury of the Corinthians, and two vessels for sprinkling water, of gold the one, and of silver the other.  On the gold bowl are written these words: "This the Lacedæmonians offered to the god."

20  17. But these words are not true, for a certain man of Delphi (whose name, though it be known, shall not be mentioned in this place) engraved them, thinking to please the Lacedæmonians.  Yet the boy, through whose hand the water flows, is an offering of the Lace- 25 dæmonians, but of the vessels themselves neither the one nor the other.

18.  Other offerings of no great account did Crœsus send to Delphi.  Yet of one must mention be made; to wit, the golden statue of a woman three cubits in 30 height.  This the men of Delphi affirm to be the like- ness of the breadcutter of King Crœsus.  Also the King offered to the god the necklace of his wife and her

girdles also.   He sent gifts likewise to the temple of Amphiaraüs.

19. Now Crœsus gave commandment to the Lydians that carried these offerings for him to Delphi and to the temple of Amphiaraüs, that they should inquire of [5] the oracles whether or no he should make war against the Persians, and whether he should seek to gain for himself any allies that should help him.

20. So when the Lydians that had been sent on this errand were come, they inquired of the oracles, saying, [10] "Crœsus, king of the Lydians, and of other nations, holding these to be the only truth-speaking oracles that are among men, sendeth to you gifts that are worthy of your wisdom, and would now inquire of you whether he shall make war against the Persians, and also in what [15] nations he shall seek for allies for himself."

21. These are the things that the messengers of Crœsus inquired of the oracles, and the two agreed together in their answers; for first they said, "If Crœsus make war against the Persians, he shall bring to the [20] ground a great empire," and next they counseled him to find out who of the Greeks were the most powerful at that season, and to make them his allies.

22. This answer rejoiced the King exceedingly, for he made sure that he should bring the empire of Cyrus [25] and the Persians to the ground.   Wherefore he sent again to Delphi, and gave to every man two gold pieces, having first inquired how many men there were in the city; for which bounty the people of Delphi gave in return to him and all other Lydians that they should [30] have first approach to the oracle, and should be free of

---

1. The rich gifts here enumerated were still in the temple treasuries in the time of Herodotus, and could be seen by visitors.

tribute, and should have the chief seat at feasts and games.  Also that any man of Lydia might, if he so willed, be free of the city of Delphi.

23. After he had bestowed this bounty on the men of
5 Delphi, Crœsus inquired of the oracle the third time; for now that he had assured himself that it spake the truth, he was instant in using it.  Therefore he inquired of it again; and this time he would fain know whether his kingdom should remain for many years.

10    24. To this the oracle answered these words—

> "Man of Lydia, when the mule
>   O'er the Medians' land shall rule,
>   Think of name and fame no more,
>   Fly by Hermus' stony shore."

15 And Crœsus, when he heard these words, was yet more exceedingly delighted, for he said to himself, "Surely now a mule shall never be king of the Medes in the place of a man.  Wherefore this kingdom shall abide to me and my children after me for ever."

20    25. After this he inquired what city of the Greeks was the most powerful at that season; and he found that there were two cities excelling in strength; to wit, Athens and Sparta, but that of these the city of Athens was much troubled by strife within itself, but that
25 Sparta was prosperous exceedingly, and had of late years subdued unto itself the greater part of the island of Pelops, in which island it is.

26. For these causes he sent messengers to Sparta with gifts, who spake after this manner, "Crœsus, king
30 of Lydia and of other nations, hath sent us, saying, 'Men of Lacedæmon, the god, even Apollo, hath com-

---

7. **Instant in using it:** He made immediate, pressing use of it.

manded me that I should make to myself friends of the Greeks, whomsoever I should find to be the strongest. Now, therefore, seeing that I find you to be the chiefest people in Greece, I do the bidding of the oracle, and come to you, and would have you for my friends and allies in all honesty and good faith.'"

27. These words King Crœsus spake by the mouth of his messengers. And the thing pleased the Lacedæmonians well, for they also had heard the words of the oracle; and they made a treaty with Crœsus, and confirmed their friendship and alliance with an oath.

28. And indeed there had been certain kindnesses done to their city by King Crœsus aforetime. For they had sent messengers to Sardis to buy gold for a certain statue that they would make; but when they sought to buy it, Crœsus gave it to them for a gift. For this cause the Lacedæmonians made alliance with Crœsus; also they were well pleased that he had chosen them out of all the Greeks to be his friends.

29. So they made themselves ready to help him when he should call upon them; and they prepared a mixing bowl of brass, wrought on the outside of it with divers figures of beasts about the brim. This bowl held three hundred firkins; and the Lacedæmonians thought fit to give it to Crœsus in return for the things that he had given to them.

30. Now the bowl came never to Sardis; but as to why it came not some say one thing and some say another. The Lacedæmonians say indeed that when the men that had charge of it were near to the island of Samos, the Samians came forth with ships of war, and assailed them, and took away the bowl from them.

31. But the men of Samos say that they who had

charge of it, when they found that the time had passed, Sardis being now taken by Cyrus, sold the bowl in Samos, and that certain persons bought it and offered it for an offering in the temple of Heré.  Perchance the 5 truth of the matter is this, that the men sold it indeed, yet affirmed when they were returned to Sparta that the Samians had taken it by force.  And this is the story of the bowl.

32. After these things Crœsus marched with a great 10 army into the land of Cappadocia, not reading the oracle aright, but hoping that he should bring to the ground the power of Cyrus and the Persians.  And while he was yet making preparations for war there came to him a certain man of Lydia whose name was 15 Sandanis.  The man had been before accounted wise, but thenceforth had such renown for wisdom among the Lydians as had none beside.

33. The man spake thus, "O King, the men against whom thou art preparing to make war have tunics of 20 leather, and all their other garments also are of leather, and for food they have not what they would but what they can get, and the country wherein they dwell is rocky and barren.  Also they use not wine, but drink water only; nor have they figs to eat, nor indeed any 25 good thing.

34. "If therefore, O King, thou shalt conquer these men, what wilt thou take from them, for indeed they have nothing.  But if they should prevail over thee, think what good things thou wilt lose.  For when they

---

12. This famous king is known as "Cyrus the Elder" and "Cyrus the Great."  In the Bible he is called *Koresh.*  He reigned from 559 B.C. to 5:9 B.C., and is regarded as the founder of the Persian Empire.  The Cyrus whose famous rebellion is described in Xenophon's *Anabasis* is known as "Cyrus the Younger."

have once tasted our good things they will hold fast by them, nor wilt thou drive them away. As for me, I thank the Gods that they have not put it into the hearts of the Persians to march against the land of Lydia." For it was so that the Persians before they conquered the Lydians had no good things of their own. For all that Sandanis prevailed not with King Crœsus to turn him from his purpose.

---

## CHAPTER III.

### KING CRŒSUS IS DEFEATED AND THE CITY OF SARDIS IS TAKEN.

1. KING CRŒSUS, being steadfastly purposed to make war with the Persians, marched into the land of the Cappadocians, wherein is the river Halys, being the boundary between his kingdom and the kingdom of Cyrus. Now the reasons that King Crœsus had for making war were these.

2. First, he desired to enlarge the borders of his dominion, adding thereto the land of the Persians ; and next, he had it in his heart to avenge upon Cyrus his sister's husband Astyages ; for Cyrus had subdued him, and taken from him his kingdom, as shall be told hereafter.

3. But how it came to pass that Crœsus was brother-in-law to Astyages shall be told at this present. Certain families of the wandering Scythians, being at variance with their own people, fled into the land of the Medes, the king of the Medes in those days being Cyax-

ares, the son of Phraortes. This Cyaxares at the first dealt kindly with these Scythians, as being men who were suppliants for his grace. And indeed he made so much of them that he put with them certain children 5 who should learn their language and the art of shooting with the bow, in which they excel.

4. Now the Scythians were wont to go hunting every day, and failed not to bring home venison ; but after a while, on a certain day it chanced that they brought 10 home nothing. And when King Cyaxares saw them returning with empty hands he was wroth with them, and entreated them shamefully, being indeed a man of violent temper.

5. Then the Scythians bethought them how they 15 might avenge themselves for this dishonor ; whereupon they took one of the children whom they were teaching, and cut him into pieces, and dressed the flesh as they were wont to dress the venison which they took in hunting, and gave it to the King as if it were some 20 wild beast which they had slain.

6. But so soon as they had given it they fled to Alyattes at Sardis ; and Cyaxares and his guests eat of the meat which had been prepared in this fashion. Now when the King heard how the Scythians had dealt with 25 him, he sent to Alyattes and demanded that they should be given over to him for punishment, but Alyattes would not.

7. After this there was war between the Lydians and the Medes for five years ; and in this war the Lydians 30 oftentimes had the advantage, and the Medes also oftentimes. But when they had fought against each other

___

12. **Entreated, etc.:** Treated, or dealt with them shamefully. This is the old use of the word.

with equal fortune for five years, it so befell that in the sixth year, when they joined battle for the first time, the day became dark as the night.   And this change of day into night Thales, of Miletus had foretold, and indeed had appointed for it the selfsame year wherein it 5 happened.

8. But when the Lydians and the Medes saw what had befallen, they were the more eager to make peace the one with the other ; and they that brought about this agreement were Syennesis of Cilicia, and Laby- 10 netus of Babylon.   These caused that the two kings should make a treaty the one with the other, and should confirm it with an oath.

9. Moreover, they made a covenant that Alyattes should give his daughter Aryenis to the son of Cyaxares 15 to wife, and this son was Astyages ; for they knew that such treaties stand not firm without there be some bond by which they that make them are bound.   As for these nations they make oaths in the same fashion as do the Greeks ; only they add this, that they make a cutting 20 upon their arms, and they lick up the blood each man from the arm of the other.

10. When Crœsus with his army was come to the river Halys, he was in great doubt how he should cross it.   But Thales of Miletus, who chanced to be in the 25 camp of the King, contrived a device by which it was done.   For he caused that the river, which before had

---

4. **Thales** (tha'leez :) Thales was one of the "seven sages " of Greece and one of the founders of the study of philosophy and mathematics.   It is thought that he obtained his knowledge of mathematics and astronomy from the Egyptians; but that he could predict an eclipse is matter of much doubt.   The Medes and Lydians were not as far advanced in scientific knowledge as the Greeks, and were therefore easily terrified by an eclipse.

10. **Syennesis** (si-en'ne-sis): This was the common name or title of the kings of Cilicia, like the title *Pharaoh* in Egypt.

10. **Labynetus** (lab-i-ne'tus): The Greek name of Nebuchadnezzar and of Belshazzar.

flowed on the left hand of the army, should flow upon the right hand.

11. And this he did by digging a deep ditch into which the river was turned before it came to the place 5 where the army was encamped ; and this, being made of the shape of a crescent, was carried in the rear of the army, and so was brought again into the river. Thus was the stream of the Halys divided between the river and the ditch; and being divided it could easily be 10 crossed.

12. Some stories say that the river was wholly dried up, all the water flowing into the ditch. But this is altogether incredible, for if the whole river had been turned into the ditch, how could King Crœsus with his 15 army have crossed it when he returned from the battle with Cyrus to Sardis ?

13. And indeed it is scarcely to be believed that the river was so turned, though this story be commonly told among the Greeks, who say that there were no 20 bridges over the Halys in those days, but rather it is to be believed that there were bridges, and that the King led his army across by them.

14. When Crœsus had crossed the Halys he came to a city of Cappadocia that was called Pterium; and this 25 Pterium was the biggest and strongest city of those parts, lying as near as may be over against Sinope, which is on the Black Sea. This city Crœsus took by assault, and sold all the dwellers therein for slaves, and took also all the towns thereof, and removed out of the 30 place where they dwelt all the people, though indeed they had done him no wrong.

---

26. **Sinope** (sĭ-no′pe): Still an important city. The ancient town has been completely ruined, and the modern town built of its fragments.

15. When Cyrus heard that King Crœsus was come against him, he also gathered his army together and went to meet him, taking with him as many as dwelt on the way by which he marched.   But before that he set out he sent out heralds to the Ionians, bidding them 5 revolt from Crœsus, whom indeed they served unwillingly ; but the Ionians would not hearken to him.

16. Cyrus therefore came up and pitched his camp over against the camp of the Lydians, which was near

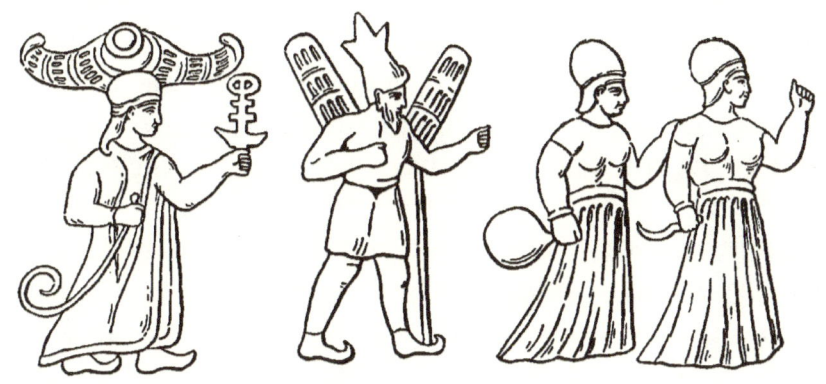

SCULPTURES FROM PTERIUM.

to the city of Pterium ; and after a while the two kings 10 joined battle.   And the battle waxed hot, and many were slain on both sides, but neither gained the advantage ; and when it was night they separated perforce.

17. But Crœsus was ill content with the number of his army, for it was less by many thousands than the army 15 of Cyrus.   For which reason on the next day, seeing that Cyrus came not forth from his camp to assail him, he departed with all haste, returning to Sardis, for he had it in his mind to call the Egyptians to his help, according to his covenant with them, for he had made alliance 20

with Amasis king of Egypt before he made alliance with the Lacedæmonians.

18. Also he would send for help to the men of Babylon, for with these also he had alliance ; and in those 5 days Labynetus was king of Babylon.   Lastly he sent a summons to the Lacedæmonians that they should send an army to him at the appointed time.   For his purpose was that he should gather together all these his allies, and should also collect as great an army as might 10 be of his own people, and so, when the winter was past, and the spring was come again, should march against the Persians.

19. Having therefore these thoughts in his heart, so soon as he came to Sardis he sent heralds to Babylon, 15 and to Egypt, and to Sparta, saying that they should send each of them an army to him at Sardis in the fifth month from that time ; but as for the soldiers that he had hired with money, these he sent away, suffering them to be altogether scattered, for it did not so much 20 as enter his thoughts that Cyrus, seeing that he had not done more than fight with him on equal terms, would march against Sardis.

20. Now while he was busy considering these things there befell this marvel, that the whole space before the 25 city was filled with serpents, and that so soon as the serpents were seen there the horses, leaving their accustomed pasture, fell to and devoured them.   This thing Crœsus held to be a portent, as indeed it was ; and straightway he sent messengers to Telmessus, where 30 there are those that interpret such things.

---

1. **Amasis** (a-ma'sis): During this king's reign the Greeks and Egyptians were brought into close and friendly intercourse with each other.
29. **Telmessus** (tel-mes'sus): A city in Caria (ka'rĭ-a), celebrated for the great number of soothsayers among its inhabitants.

21. But these messengers, though indeed they went to Telmessus and heard from the interpreters what the meaning of this portent might be, were not able to show the matter to the King; for before that they came back to Sardis King Crœsus had been vanquished 5 and taken prisoner.

22. But the meaning of the portent according to the interpreters of Telmessus was this, " Let Crœsus look to see an army of strangers in his land ; and let him know that when this army is come to his land it will 10 subdue the inhabitants thereof ; for the serpent is a son of the land, but the horse is a stranger and an enemy."

23. This was the answer of the interpreters of Telmessus ; and they made it when Crœsus was already 15 vanquished, but they knew nothing of that which had befallen Sardis and the king thereof.

24. But so soon as Crœsus had departed after the battle at Pterium, Cyrus, knowing that he had it in his thought to scatter his army, judged that he should do 20 well if he marched straightway against Sardis before that the Lydians could gather themselves together against him a second time. And this thing he did without delay. For he marched into the land of Lydia with all haste ; nor did Crœsus receive any message of 25 his coming before that he saw the King himself with his army.

25. Then was Crœsus sorely perplexed, for the matter had turned out wholly against his expectations. Nevertheless he took heart and led out the Lydians to battle. 30 And indeed in those days there was not in the whole land of Asia any nation that was more stalwart and valiant than the nation of the Lydians. The people

were accustomed to fight from horseback, carrying long
spears, nor were there any horsemen more skillful.

26. The Lydians therefore and the Persians were ar-
rayed one against the other in the plain that lieth be-
5 fore Sardis, and this plain is very great and wholly bare
of trees. But when Cyrus saw the array of the Lydians
he was afraid of their horsemen, so many and well
equipped were they.

27. Then a certain Mede, Harpagus by name, coun-
10 seled him what he should do, and Cyrus hearkened to
him. He took all the camels that followed his army,
carrying victuals and baggage, and taking their burdens
from them, set riders upon them, arming all of them
as horsemen. And having so furnished the camels, he
15 commanded that they should go before his army against
the horsemen of Crœsus. And behind the camels he
put the foot soldiers, and behind the foot soldiers the
horsemen.

28. And when the whole army was drawn up in
20 battle array, he straightway commanded them that they
should slay all else of the Lydians who might fall in
their way, but that Crœsus himself they should not
slay, not even if he should defend himself when they
laid hands upon him.

25  29. Now the reason why he set the camels in array
against the horsemen was this. The horse is sore afraid
of the camel, and cannot endure to look upon the shape
of the beast or to smell the smell. For this cause therefore he used this device, that the King of the Lydians
30 might find no gain from his horsemen, by whom he
hoped that he should win a great victory.

30. And indeed so soon as ever the two armies had
joined battle, and the horses smelled the smell of the

camels and saw them, they turned and fled.  So was Crœsus utterly disappointed of his hope.

31. Nevertheless the Lydians bare themselves bravely; for when they saw what had befallen them, they leapt from their horses and fought with the Persians on foot. 5 But after a while, when many had been slain on both sides, the Lydians were driven into their city, and were besieged therein by the Persians.

32. Now it seemed to Crœsus that the siege would be of many months.  Therefore he sent again other mes- 10 sengers to his allies saying that, whereas he had before bidden them to assemble themselves at Sardis in the fifth month, there was now need that they should come with all the speed that might be, for that the King was besieged. ·                                                     15

33. Now of the other allies nothing need be said ; but as to the Lacedæmonians, when the messengers of Crœsus came to them, they were at variance with their neighbors, the men of Argos.  Notwithstanding, they made all haste to come to the help of the King ; and 20 were indeed ready to set forth, with ships duly furnished, when there came to them tidings that the city of Sardis was taken and Crœsus led into captivity. When they heard this they changed their purpose and went not ;  nevertheless they thought it a grievous 25 thing.

34. Now the taking of Sardis was in this wise.  On the fourteenth day after the beginning of the siege, Cyrus sent horsemen throughout his army, saying that he would give great gifts to the man who should first 30 mount upon the wall.

35. But when the whole army had attacked the city, and prevailed nothing, a certain Mardian, whose name

was Hyrœades, desisted not as did the others, but made his attempt on a certain part of the citadel where no sentinels were set. And none were set because no man had any fear that the citadel could be taken from this 5 quarter, for the place was very steep. And this indeed was the only part of the citadel to which Meles, who had been king of Sardis in old time, had not caused the lion's cub to be carried.

36. Now the story of the lion's cub is this. A woman 10 in Sardis brought forth a young lion, and the interpreters of Telmessus said, "If thou carry the young lion round about its wall, no man shall take Sardis." So Meles caused them to carry the cub round about the wall wherever it could be attacked, but of this place 15 he took no account, so steep was it and hard of access.

37. Now Hyrœades had seen on the day before that a certain Lydian had come down by this place after a helmet that had rolled down from the top, and had fetched 20 the helmet, and so returned. And having seen this thing he bare it in mind; and the next day he climbed up the same way, and many Persians after him.

38. So Sardis was taken and all the city plundered. As to the King himself, there befell this thing that shall 25 now be told. He had a son, of whom indeed mention has been made before. A goodly youth he was in all other respects, but he was dumb. Now in the days of his prosperity Crœsus, having done many other things that the youth might be healed of his infirmity, sent 30 also messengers to the oracle of Delphi to inquire of the god.

---

1. **Hyrœades** (hi-re'a-deez): The Mardi or Amardi were a powerful, warlike tribe from near the Caspian Sea.

39. To these the Pythia made answer in these words—

> "O king of many lands, the thought
>   Thou keepest in thy heart is vain:
> The help with many prayers besought
>   Think not to ask of heaven again;
> For ill the day and full of fear
> That first thy dumb child's voice shall hear."

5

40. Now it came to pass that when the Persians were taking the citadel, one of them made as if he would have slain Crœsus, not knowing who he was. And Crœsus, though he saw the man coming against him, heeded him not, so great was his trouble; for he thought that it would be well for him to die.

41. But the youth, that had been dumb all his days, when he saw the Persian about to strike, by reason of his fear and of the instant necessity of the thing, cried out, saying, "Fellow, slay not King Crœsus." Thus did he speak for the first time; but afterward, for the rest of his life, he spake even as other men.

10

15

———— •

## CHAPTER IV.

CRŒSUS IS SAVED FROM DEATH.  OF LYDIA, THE LYD-
    IANS, AND OF CERTAIN GREEKS THAT DWELT IN
    ASIA.

1. So the Persians gained possession of the city of Sardis. And Crœsus himself they took alive, and led him to Cyrus their king; and all the years that he had reigned were fourteen; fourteen also was the number of the days for which his city was besieged. And thus

20

was the prophecy of the oracle fulfilled, that he should bring to an end a great empire; to wit, his own.

2. Then Cyrus commanded that they should build a great pile of wood, and should set Crœsus thereon bound 5 in chains, and with him fourteen men of Lydia, and burn them with fire. But whether in so doing he thought to offer the first-fruits of his victory to some god, or was performing a vow which he had made, or, having heard that Crœsus had been a great worshipper 10 of the Gods, desired now to see whether any god would come and help him in his need, cannot certainly be known.

3. But when Crœsus stood upon the pile, and the fire had now been put to it, there came into his thoughts, 15 notwithstanding the great strait wherein he stood, that the saying of Solon was indeed true, and spoken by inspiration of the Gods, when he said that none of living men might be counted happy. And when he thought of this he cried out with a loud voice, having before 20 kept silence altogether, "Solon, Solon, Solon!" which when Cyrus heard, he bade the interpreters ask of Crœsus who was this that he called upon.

4. But when the interpreters asked this thing, for a time Crœsus kept silence, but afterward, for indeed he 25 was constrained to speak, made this answer, "He is one with whom it would be better than many possessions for all rulers to have speech." Then, as no man could understand these words, they inquired of him again what they might signify.

30 5. And as they were earnest with him, and would not leave him in peace, he told them how there had come to his court one Solon, a man of Athens, who, having seen all his wealth and prosperity, had made little account

of it; and how that there had befallen him all that this
same Solon had said, though indeed the man spake not

CRŒSUS ON THE FUNERAL PILE.

of him in particular but of all mortal men, and especially of those who judged themselves to be happy.

6. This was the answer which Crœsus made; and now the pile had been lighted, and the extremities were
on fire. But when Cyrus heard from the interpreters
the words of Crœsus, he repented him of his purpose,
bethinking him how that he, being but a mortal man,
was now giving another man that had aforetime been
not less prosperous than himself to be burned with fire,
and fearing lest there should come upon him vengeance
for such a deed, and considering also that there was
nothing sure in human affairs.

7. For which reasons he bade them that stood by
quench the fire and cause Crœsus and the men that
were with him to descend from the pile. But these,
with all their striving, could not prevail over the fire.
Then Crœsus—for this is the story of the Lydians—
when he saw that Cyrus had repented him of his pur-

pose, and that every one was striving to quench the fire but could not, cried with a loud voice to Apollo, beseeching the god that if he had ever made an offering that was to his liking, he would deliver him from his 5 present peril.

8. This he besought of the god with many tears, and lo! of a sudden, though the day before had been fine and calm, there came a great storm with a most vehement rain, which quenched the fire. Then Cyrus knew 10 of a surety that Crœsus was a good man and dear to the Gods. And having caused him to descend from the pile, he asked him, saying, " Tell me, Crœsus, what man persuaded thee to lead thy army against my land, and to make me thine enemy, having been before thy 15 friend ?"

9. Then Crœsus answered, " This I did, O King, for thy good fortune, but to my loss. Nor was it a man that did this, but the gods of the Greeks, who encouraged me to make war against thee. For surely no man 20 is so foolish that of his own will he should choose war instead of peace; for in peace the children bury their fathers, but in war the fathers bury their children. But these things have fallen out as the Gods would have them."

25　10. When he had said these things Cyrus bade them loose his chains, and put him near to himself, and marveled when he regarded him, both he and the Persians that were with him. And Crœsus said nothing, thinking about many things. But after a while, when he 30 saw the Persians plundering the city of the Lydians, he turned him to King Cyrus, and said, "Is it allowed to me, O King, to speak that which is in my heart, or

shall I be silent?"   And Cyrus bade him be of courage
and speak what he would.

11. Then Crœsus asked him, " What is it that this
great multitude is so busy about ?"   " They are spoiling
thy city," said Cyrus, " and carrying off thy posses- 5
sions."   " Nay," said Crœsus, " this is not my city that
they spoil, nor my possessions that they carry off; for
I have now no share or lot in these things.   But the
things that they plunder are thine."

12. Then Cyrus took heed of the words which Crœsus 10
had spoken to him; and bidding all others leave him,
he asked him again what he thought of these matters.

13. Then Crœsus made answer, "The Gods have
made me thy servant; wherefore I count it right to tell
thee if I perceive aught that thou seest not.   The Per- 15
sians are haughty by nature, but they are poor.   And if
thou sufferest them to plunder in this fashion and to
gain for themselves great wealth, be sure that this will
befall thee.   That man among them who shall get the
most will be he that will rebel against thee.   If there- 20
fore my words please thee, do according to my bidding.
Set spearmen as guards at all the gates, and let them
take away from all that come out the things that they
carry with them, saying at the same time, ' We must
needs give tithe to Zeus of all these things.'   And they 25
will not hate thee as if thou didst take the things from
them by force, but will judge thee to do that which is
right, and will give them up willingly."

14. When Cyrus heard these words he was pleased
with them beyond measure, judging them to have been 30
wisely said.   So when he had commended Crœsus for
his wisdom, and had given commandment to the spearmen according to these words, he said, " Thou hast it in

thy heart to do good deeds and to say good words as be-
fitteth a king; ask therefore some boon of me which
thou wouldest have granted to thee straightway."

15. Then said Crœsus, " O King, thou canst not please
5 me more, than if thou wilt suffer me to send to the god
of the Greeks, whom I have honored with gifts more
than all Gods beside, and to lay these fetters before
him, and ask him whether it is his custom to deceive
them that do him honor."

10  16. And when Cyrus would know why he desired to
put this question accusing the god, Crœsus set before
him the whole matter, both that which he had asked,
and the answer of the god, and the offerings which he
had made, and how he had made war against the Per-
15 sians, being encouraged thereto by the god.

17. And when he had ended this tale he besought
Cyrus again that he would suffer him to reproach the
god with these things.  And Cyrus, when he heard it,
laughed and said, " This request I grant thee, O Crœsus,
20 as I will grant thee everything that thou shalt ask me
hereafter."

18. And when Crœsus heard these words he sent certain Lydians to Delphi, and bade them lay the fetters on
the threshold of the temple and inquire of the god
25 whether he was not ashamed to have encouraged Crœsus
by his oracles to march against the Persians, thinking
that he should overthrow the empire of Cyrus, of which
undertaking these, the fetters to wit, were the first-
fruits, and whether it was the custom of the god of the
30 Greeks to be unfaithful.

19. And when the Lydians did as had been commanded them, the Pythia made this answer, " That
which is fated it is by no means possible to avoid, not

even to a god.   And Crœsus hath suffered for the trans-
gressions of his forefather in the fifth generation, who,
being a body-guard of the king, slew his master, a
woman helping him with her craft, and took his honor
to himself, though he had no part or lot in it.            5

20. "And Apollo was very earnest with the Fates
that they should not bring this evil upon Sardis in the
days of Crœsus, but that they should bring it in his son's
days.   Yet could he not prevail.   Nevertheless all that
the Fates granted to him that did he for Crœsus, delay- 10
ing the taking of Sardis for the space of three years;
for let Crœsus be sure of this, that the taking of Sardis
is later by three years than had been ordained at the
first.   Also when he was in peril of being burnt with
fire the god helped him and delivered him.                 15

21. "And as for the oracle, Crœsus doth not right to
blame him, for Apollo foretold to him that, if he should
make war against the Persians, he should bring to the
ground a great empire.   If therefore he had been well
advised in this matter, he should have sent again to in- 20
quire of the god whether his own empire or the empire
of Cyrus were thus signified.

22. "But seeing that he understood not the thing
which was said, nor inquired a second time, let him
blame himself.   And as to that which Apollo answered 25
him when he inquired of him the last time, speaking of
a mule, this also Crœsus understood not.   For Cyrus
was this mule, being born of parents that were not of
the same race, his mother also being of the more noble

---

6. **Fates:** The Fates, or Destinies, were goddesses who were believed to
preside over the birth, life, and death of human beings.   There names were
Clotho (klo'-tho), Lachesis (lak'e-sis), and Atropos (at'ro-pos); they are represented as spinning the thread of life from the distaff.   Find, if possible,
Michael Angelo's picture of the Fates, or Parcæ.

stock and his father of the worse.   For she was a woman
of the Medes and the daughter of King Astyages, and
he was a Persian and no king, but a servant that married the daughter of his master."

5    23. This was the answer that the priestess gave to the
Lydians; and when Crœsus heard it he confessed that
he had erred and not the god.

24. In this way did the empire of the Lydians come
to an end.   These Lydians were the first that found
10 out the coining of gold and silver.   Also they were the
first traders.   And they say of themselves that they first
made the games at which they and the Greeks are used
to play.   Also they declare that in the days when these
games were first made by them they colonized the land
15 of Tyrsenia, which is in Italy.

25. And their story of this matter is this.   In the
days of Atys the son of Manes there was a sore famine
throughout the whole land of Lydia.   And for a while
the Lydians were instant in prayers to the Gods that
20 they would help them; but, as the famine ceased not,
they sought for remedies contriving some one thing
and some another.

26. In those days they devised dice-playing and ball-
playing and all other kinds of games that men use, save
25 chess only, for this the Lydians say not that they devised.   And their manner with the games was this.
One day they would play continually, that they might
not have any thought for food, and the next day they
would leave off from their playing and eat.

---

17. **Manes** (ma'neez): Manes was king of the Mæonians; his grandson,
the son of Atys (a'tis). was Lydus (li'dus), after whom the Mæonians were
called Lydians.   Tyrsenus (tĭr-se'nus), or Tyrrhenus, was the brother of
Lydus.

24. **Ball-playing :** Plato tells us that the game of ball was invented in
Egypt, where it was certainly used as early as 2000 B.C.

27. In this fashion they endured for the space of eighteen years. But as the evil abated not but rather grew worse, the King divided the people of Lydia into two parts, making them cast lots, that the one part should remain in the land, and the other part should go forth to some other country. And that part which drew the lot for remaining he took to himself, but that part which should go forth he gave to his son, whose name was Tyrsenus.

28. These men went down to the seacost, to Smyrna, and there built them ships, into which they put all things that they needed for a voyage, and so set sail, seeking for livelihood and a country wherein they might dwell; in which search, having passed by many lands, they came to the land of the Umbri, and there built for themselves cities, in the which they dwell to this day. Also they changed their name, calling themselves no more Lydians but Tyrsenians, after the name of the King's son, Tyrsenus, who had led them forth.

29. Now the men of Ionia and Æolia, so soon as they knew that the Lydians had been subdued by the Persians, sent messengers to Cyrus, saying that they would fain be his servants after the same manner in which they had been the servants of Crœsus.

30. But when they had made their oration to him he spake to them for an answer this parable. "A certain flute-player, seeing fishes in the sea, played his flute to them, thinking that they would come forth from the sea on to the land at his playing. But when they would not do as he had hoped, he took a net, and cast it, and having encompassed therewith a great multitude of fishes, he drew it to the land. And when he saw them that they flapped their tails upon the ground, he said,

'Cease this dancing, for ye would not come out and dance upon the land when I piped to you.'"

31. This said Cyrus because in the beginning of the war he had sent to these men bidding them rebel against
5 Crœsus, and they would not, but now when they knew that he had gotten himself the victory, they were ready to be his servants. For this cause he was very wroth with them; and when the men of Ionia and Æolia heard his words, they knew that he purposed evil against
10 them, and began to prepare themselves accordingly.

32. First they sent messengers to Sparta to ask for help; who, when they were come, chose Pythermus, a man of Phocæa, to speak for them. This Pythermus, having clad himself in purple, which he did that all the
15 Spartans might come together to see him, stood up in the assembly, and told his business. But the Spartans consented not to help; only after that the messengers had departed they sent certain men in a ship of fifty oars, who should see for themselves how things were
20 with Cyrus and the Ionians.

33. The chief of these men, a certain Lacrines, went up to Sardis, and declared to Cyrus the pleasure of the Lacedæmonians, that he should not harm any city of the Greeks, for that they would not suffer it. But when
25 Cyrus heard these words he inquired of certain Greeks that were with him, what manner of men and how many in number these Lacedæmonians might be that they laid such commands upon him.

34. And when he heard he said to Lacrines, "I re-
30 gard not at all the folk who have a set place in the midst of their city whither they assemble and forswear themselves and deceive each other. Surely, if it be well with me, all that the Ionians have suffered they shall

suffer." Cyrus said this reproaching the Greeks because they have markets wherein they buy and sell, for
the Persians use not to do any such thing.

35. After this Cyrus departed, and took Crœsus with
him; and over Sardis and the Lydians he made a cer- 5
tain Persian, named Tabalus, governor, but the charge
of the gold he gave to Pactyas, a man of Lydia. But
Pactyas took the gold, and having hired soldiers besieged Tabalus in the citadel of Sardis.

36. When tidings of these things were brought to 10
Cyrus as he journeyed eastward, he changed not his
purpose, having weightier things in hand, but sent Mazares a Mede with a part of the army to deal with the
Lydians and Ionians. Of whose coming when Pactyas
heard he escaped from the citadel of Sardis and fled to 15
Cumæ. Whereupon Mazares sent messengers to Cumæ,
bidding the inhabitants deliver up the enemy of the
King.

37. But the men of Cumæ doubted what they should
do, and sent messengers to inquire of the god in Bran- 20
chidæ of Miletus; to whom the god answered that they
should deliver up Pactyas. But when this answer was
brought back, and the people were now ready to deliver
him up, the thing pleased not one of the chief men,
Aristodicus by name, who persuaded the men of Cumæ 25
that they should send yet again and inquire of the god
by the hand of other messengers.

38. So they sent other messengers, among whom was

---

3. **Use not to do**: Are not in the habit of doing. The Persians of the
nobler class would neither buy nor sell at all, since they would be supplied
by their dependents and through presents with all that they required for
the common purposes of life. Only those of the lower rank would buy at
shops, which were not allowed in the Forum, or public place of meeting.
7. **Pactyas** (pak'tĭ-as): Pactyas was charged by Cyrus to collect the
treasure of the kingdom and bring it after him.

Aristodicus himself.    When they were come to the oracle, Aristodicus, being spokesman for the rest, spake, saying, " O King, there came to us a certain Pactyas, a man of Lydia, flying from the Persians, who were ready 5 to put him to death.    And now these Persians will have us deliver him to them.    But we, though we fear them, are yet loath to deliver the man to death, and so are come asking thee what we should do."

39.  To this the god answered again that they should 10 deliver him up.    But when Aristodicus heard this he went about the temple taking the young birds out of their nests, for many birds had built therein.    As he did this there came a voice out of the shrine, " What doest thou, thou wicked man, taking these that have 15 sought sanctuary with me ?"

40.  Then Aristodicus answered, " O King, thou indeed defendest them that seek sanctuary with thee, but thou biddest the men of Cumæ deliver up this suppliant." And the god answered, " Yea, I bade you do this thing, 20 that so ye might perish utterly, and might not ask such ill questions of the god any more."

41.  When the men of Cumæ heard these words they neither were willing to deliver him up nor to keep him, and so be besieged.    Therefore they sent him to Mity- 25 lene.    But when they knew that the men of Mitylene were preparing to deliver him up for a reward, they sent a ship and took him to Chios; but the Chians delivered him up to the Persians, receiving for him a certain place called Atarnes, which is in Mysia, over against 30 Lesbos.    And to this day Atarnes is accursed, and the Chians use not any of its fruits for sacrifice.

42.  After this Tabalus, having subdued certain cities of Ionia, died, and Cyrus sent Harpagus a Mede, of

wnom there is much to be said hereafter, to be captain in his room.    And the first city which Harpagus made ready to attack was Phocæa.    Now the men of Phocæa were mighty sailors, and were the first of the Greeks to make long voyages, visiting, besides other places, Tar- 5 tessus, which is in Spain.

43.  Now in Tartessus they found a certain king whose name was Arganthonius.    He was a very old man of sixscore years, and he had reigned in Tartessus fourscore years.    This Arganthonius dealt very kindly with the 10 Phocæans, and when he knew that the power of the Medes waxed great in Asia, gave them much money that they might build them a wall; which wall indeed they built of great stones well fitted together.

44.  Now when Harpagus was come to Phocæa, he 15 sent messengers bidding them submit themselves to Cyrus; and he said that it would suffice if they would throw down one battlement on their wall, and set apart one house in their city.    But the men of Phocæa asked for one day that they might deliberate, and would have 20 Harpagus take his army from before their city for so long.

45.  Then said Harpagus, " I know well what ye purpose to do, yet shall ye have the day."    And he took his army from before the city.    Then the Phocæans 25 launched their ships, and put therein their wives and children and their goods, and all the images from the temples, and all the offerings, save such as were of brass or stone, or pictures; and having done this they sailed to Chios; and the Persians took Phocæa, being 30 deserted of its inhabitants.

---

5. **Tartessus :** The same as *Tarsus* and *Tarshish*, a colony founded very early by the Phœnicians, near modern Cadiz.

46. But the Phocæans would fain have bought certain islands of the people of Chios, but these would not sell them, fearing lest they should suffer in trading. Then they sailed to Cyrnus, where twenty years before 5 they had built a city. But first they sailed back to Phocæa and slew the garrison which Harpagus had set there to keep it; and having slain the garrison, they threw an anvil of iron into the sea, and sware that they would not return to the city till they should see the 10 anvil floating on the water.

47. Yet, while they were voyaging to Cyrnus, half and more repented them of their purpose, and brake their oath, and went back to Phocæa, and dwelt there. But such as kept to their oath sailed to Cyrnus, where 15 they dwelt for five years. But at the end of five years the Phœnicians and the men of Carthage made alliance and sailed against them, for they plundered all the neighboring parts. Then was there a great battle, and the Phocæans prevailed, yet lost forty ships out of three-20 score. Then those that remained sailed to Rhegium in Italy, and built a city in those parts.

48. The men of Tios did as the Phocæans had done, for they put all that they had in ships, and departed, and dwelt in a city of Thrace called Abdera. But all 25 the other Ionians on the mainland submitted themselves to Cyrus; and the islanders did likewise, fearing what might befall them.

49. After this Harpagus subdued the other nations that are in those parts, as the Carians and the Lycians

---

11. **Cyrnus** (sĭr'nus): The Greek name of Corsica.
13. Of this Herodotus says more fully: "More than half of their number were seized with such sadness and so great a longing to see once more their city and their ancient homes, that they broke the oath by which they had bound themselves and sailed back to Phocæa."

and others.    About these there is nothing worthy to be told, save about the Lycians of Xanthus only.    For these first of all fought against the Persians before their city, and being vanquished for all their valor, for they were few fighting against many, and being shut up in 5 their city, yet would not yield themselves.    For first they gathered together in their citadel their wives and their children and their slaves and all their goods, and burnt them with fire.    And having done this, they bound themselves with dreadful oaths, and fell upon 10 the Persians, and died fighting all of them.

## CHAPTER V.

### THE BIRTH AND BRINGING UP OF CYRUS.

1. ASTYAGES king of the Medes had a daughter whose name was Mandané; and of this daughter, when she was but a child, he dreamed such a dream that he feared exceedingly what might happen to him and to 15 his kingdom by reason of her.

2. Therefore when she grew of age to be married, he gave her not to a man of her own race, but he gave her to a Persian, whose name was Cambyses.    And this Cambyses was indeed of a noble house, but of a quiet 20 and peaceable temper.    Only because he was a Persian, Astyages held him to be of less account than a Mede, whether he were noble or no.

3. But in the first year of the marriage King Astyages dreamed another dream of his daughter, which 25

made him yet more afraid than had the former dream. Therefore he sent for the woman, who was now about to bring forth her first-born child, and kept her in the palace, being minded to put to death that which should 5 be born of her, for the interpreters of dreams had signified to him that the son of his daughter should be king in his stead.

4. When therefore she bare Cyrus, for they gave this name to the child, Astyages called to him one Harpagus, 10 who was of his kindred, and faithful to him beyond all other of the Medes, and who had also the care of his household. And when Harpagus was come to him, the King said, "Harpagus, see thou that in the matter which I shall now put in thy charge thou in no wise 15 neglect my commandment, nor prefer others to me, and so in the end bring great sorrow on thyself. Now the matter is this. Thou shalt take this child that Mandané my daughter hath lately borne, and carry it to thy home, and there slay it; and afterward thou shalt bury 20 it in such fashion as thou wilt."

5. To this Harpagus said, " O King, thou hast never perceived any transgression in thy servant in time past; and he will take good heed that he sin not against thee in time to come. And as for this matter of which thou 25 speakest, if thou wilt have it so, it must needs be done."

6. When Harpagus had said this, they gave him the child into his hands, the child being dressed as if for death and burial, and he took it and went to his home weeping. And when he was come thither he said to 30 his wife all the words that King Astyages had said to him.

7. Then the woman spake, saying, "What then art thou minded to do in this matter?" And he said, " Of

a surety I shall not do as the King hath commanded me. For though he should be turned aside to folly, and be stricken with madness even more grievously than he is now stricken, yet why should I be the slayer of this child? And the causes wherefore I will not do this 5 thing are many. For first he is of my own kindred, and next Astyages is an old man and hath no male offspring. If, then, when he shall die, his kingdom shall go to his daughter, whose child he biddeth me to slay, surely I shall stand in great peril. It must needs be 10 that the child die; for how else shall I escape, but the slayer shall be one of the servants of Astyages, and not I or one of my own servants."

8. When he had thus spoken, he sent a messenger straightway to one of the herdsmen of Astyages, know- 15 ing that the man dwelt in a place well fitted for the purpose, that is to say, a mountain abounding in wild beasts. The name of this herdsman was Mitradates, and his wife was a slavewoman, Spaco by name.

9. As for the pastures where he pastured his herd, 20 they lay under the mountains which are northward from Egbatana, toward the Black Sea. For this region of the land of Media is covered with woods and mountains, but the country for the most part is a plain country. The herdsman therefore being thus called came 25 with all speed.

---

22. **Egbatana** (eg-bat'a-na): The capital of Media, more commonly called *Ecbatana*. Herodotus describes it thus: "The walls are of great size and strength, rising in circles one within the other. The plan of the place is, that each of the walls should out-top the one beyond it by the battlements. The nature of the ground, which is a gentle hill, favors this arrangement in some degree, but it was mainly effected by art. The number of the circles is seven, the royal palace and the treasuries standing within the last. The circuit of the outer wall is very nearly the same with that at Athens. Of this wall the battlements are white, of the next black, of the third scarlet, of the fourth blue, of the fifth orange; all these are colored with paint. The two last have their battlements coated respectively with silver and gold."

10. And when he was come, Harpagus said to him, "Astyages bids thee take this child and put him in some desert place among the mountains that he may speedily perish. And he bids me say that if thou slay him not, but in any way sufferest him to live, he will destroy thee most miserably. And I am appointed to see that this thing be done."

11. When the herdsman heard these words he took the child and went on his way to his home, and came to the stalls of the cattle. Now it chanced that his wife had been in travail all that day, and that she bare a child while the herdsman was at the city. And the two were much troubled each about the other ; for the husband feared lest haply it should go ill with his wife in her travail, and the woman was afraid because Harpagus had sent for her husband in much haste, which thing he had not been wont to do.

12. When therefore he had returned, the woman, seeing that he was come back speedily and beyond her hope, asked of him, saying, "Why did Harpagus send for thee in such haste ?" Then the man made answer, "When I was come to the city I saw and heard such things as I would had never befallen my masters ; for the whole house of Harpagus was full of weeping and wailing. And when I went into the house, being sore astonished at these things, I saw a child lying there and crying ; and the child was adorned with gold and fine clothing.

13. "And Harpagus, so soon as he saw me, bade me take up the child with all haste and depart, and put it on such mountain as I knew to be most haunted by wild beasts. And he said that King Astyages had given commandment that this should be done. And he added

many threats of what should befall me, if I should not do as he had bidden me.

14. "Wherefore I took the child, and carried it away, thinking that it was the child of some one in the household; for the truth, as it was, I could not have 5 imagined, yet did I marvel to see that the child was adorned with gold and fine apparel, and also that there should be so great a mourning in the house of Harpagus. But as I went on my way, one of the servants of Harpagus, whom he had sent with me, recounted to me the 10 whole matter, that this child was the son of Mandané the daughter of Astyages and Cambyses the son of Cyrus, and that Astyages had given commandment that it should be slain. This therefore is the child whom thou seest."                                                    15

15. And when the herdsman had said this he took away the covering, and showed the child to his wife. And when she saw the babe, that it was fair and well-favored, she wept, and laid hold of her husband by his knees and besought him that he would not do this 20 thing, putting forth the child to die. But the man answered that he could not by any means do otherwise, for that Harpagus would send those who would see whether the thing had been done or no, and that he should perish miserably if he should be found to have 25 transgressed the commandment.

16. Then the woman, seeing that she could not prevail with her husband, spake to him again, saying, "If then I cannot prevail with thee that thou shouldest not put forth the child, yet listen to me. If the men must 30 needs see a child put forth, do thou this thing that I

---

12. This is Cyrus I., the son of Teispes, the son of Achæmenes, the founder of the Persian line of kings.

shall tell thee.   I was delivered of a child this day, and the child was dead when it was born.   Take therefore this dead child and put it forth, and let us rear this child of the daughter of Astyages as if it were our own.
5 So thou wilt not be found to transgress the commands of thy masters, and we shall also have done well for ourselves.   For indeed the dead child shall have a royal burial, and the living child shall not be slain."

17. And here the woman seemed to her husband the
10 herdsman to have spoken very wisely and seasonably, and he did according to her word.   For the child that he had brought with him that he might cause him to die, this he gave to his wife to rear ; and his own child, being dead already, he put into the basket wherein he
15 had carried the other.   With this he put all the ornaments wherewith the child had been adorned, and carried it to the most desolate place that he knew among the mountains, and there laid it forth.

18. And on the third day after he had done this, he
20 went again to the city, leaving his herds in the charge of one of them that were under him, and entering into the house of Harpagus, said he was ready to show the dead body of the child to any whom he might send. Wherefore Harpagus sent such of his own body-guard
25 as he judged to be most faithful, and saw the thing, not himself indeed, but with their eyes, and afterward buried the child that was the child of the herdsman.

19. As for the child that had afterward the name of Cyrus, the wife of the herdsman took him and reared
30 him, but called him by some other name.   When the boy was ten years old there befell a thing by which his birth was discovered.   He was wont to play with other boys that were his equals in age, in the village wherein

were the dwellings of the herdsman and his fellows. And the boys in their sport chose him, being, as was supposed, the herdsman's son, to be their king.

20. And he, being thus chosen, gave to each his proper work, setting one to build houses, and others to 5 be his body-guards, and one to be the " Eye of the King," and others to carry messages, to each his own work. Now one of the boys that played with him, being the son of one Artembares, a man of renown among the Medes, would not do the thing which Cyrus had 10 commanded him. Wherefore Cyrus bade the other boys lay hold of him ; and when these had done his bidding he corrected him for his fault with many and grievous stripes.

21. But the boy, so soon as he was let go, thinking 15 that he had suffered a grievous wrong, went in great wrath to the city and made complaint to his father of the things which he had suffered at the hands of Cyrus ; only he spake not of Cyrus, for he bare not as yet that name, but of the herdsman's son. 20

22. Then Artembares, being in a great rage, went straightway to King Astyages, taking with him his son, as one that had been shamefully entreated. And he said to the King, " See, O King, how we have been wronged by this slave who is the son of thy herdsman." 25 And he showed him the lad's shoulders, where might be seen the marks of the stripes.

23. When Astyages heard and saw these things he was ready to avenge the lad on him that had done these things, wishing to do honor to Artembares. There- 30 fore he sent for the herdsman and the boy. And when

7. **Eye of the King :** This is an Eastern expression for the king's chief officer or guard.

they were both come before him, Astyages looked
toward Cyrus, "How didst thou, being the son of this
herdsman, dare to do such shameful things to the son
of a man who is first of all them that stand before me?"
5    24. To this Cyrus made answer, "My lord, all this
that I did, I did with good cause; for the boys of the
village, this also being one of them, in their play chose
me to be their king, for I seemed to them to be the fit-
test for this honor.    All the others indeed did the
10 things which I commanded them; but this boy was dis-
obedient and paid no heed to me; for which things he
received punishment as was due.    And if thou deemest
it fit that I should suffer for so doing, lo, here I am!"

25. When the lad spake in this fashion, Astyages,
15 considering with himself the whole matter, knew him
who he was.    For the likeness of his countenance be-
trayed him; his speech also was more free than could
be looked for in the son of a herdsman, and his age also
agreed with the time of putting forth the child of his
20 daughter.

26. And being beyond measure astonished at these
things, for a while he sat speechless; but at last, having
scarcely come to himself, he said to Artembares, "Artembares, I will so deal with this matter that neither
25 thou nor thy son shall blame me," for he would have
the man go forth from his presence, that having the
herdsman alone he might question him more closely
concerning these matters.

27. Then the King sent Artembares away, and bade
30 his servants take Cyrus with them into the house.    Being therefore left alone with the herdsman, he inquired
of him, saying, "Tell me whence didst thou receive this
child, and who is he that gave him to thee?"    Then

said the herdsman, "Surely he is my son, and she that bare him is my wife, and is yet alive in my house."

28. But the King answered, "Thou answerest not well for thyself; thou wilt bring thyself into great peril." And he bade his guards lay hold upon him. But the man, when he saw that he was being led away to the tormentors, said that he would tell the whole truth. And indeed he unfolded the story from the beginning, and neither changed nor concealed anything. And when he had ended, he was earnest in prayer to the King that he would have mercy upon him and pardon him.

29. As for the herdsman indeed, when he had thus told the truth, Astyages took little heed of him; but he had great wrath against Harpagus, and sent to him by his guards that he should come forthwith. And when he was come, the King said to him, "Harpagus, how didst thou slay the boy whom I delivered to thee that was born of my daughter?"

30. And Harpagus, seeing that the herdsman stood before the King, sought not to hide the matter, for he judged that he should be easily convicted if he should speak that which was false. Therefore he said, "O King, when I took the child from thy hands, I considered with myself how I might best do thy pleasure, so that I might both be blameless before thee, and also free of blood-guiltiness as concerning thy daughter.

31. "And I did after this manner. I called this herdsman to me, and gave the child into his hands, telling him that thou hadst given commandment that it should be slain. Then I bade him take the child, and put it out in some desert place among the mountains, and watch by it till it should die. And at the same time

I used to him all manner of threats, if he should not in all things fulfil my words. And when the man had done according to my bidding, I sent the most faithful of my servants, and having seen by their eyes that the 5 child was dead, I buried him. This is the truth of the matter, O King, and in this manner the child died."

32. When Harpagus had ended this story, wherein he spake, as he thought, the whole truth, Astyages hid his anger in his heart, and related the whole matter as he 10 had heard it from the herdsman; and when it was ended, he said, "The boy yet lives; and it is well; for indeed I have been much troubled, remembering what had been done to the child; nor did I count it a light matter that my daughter was displeased with me.

15    33. "Now, therefore, that the matter hath turned out so well, first send thine own son that he may be a companion to this boy, and next come and dine with me to-day, for I would have a feast of thanksgiving for this boy that was dead and is alive again." When Harpagus 20 heard these words, he bowed himself down before the King, rejoicing beyond measure that his transgression had had so good an ending, and that he had been called to the feast of thanksgiving; and he went to his house.

34. And being come, in the joy of his heart he told 25 to his wife all that had befallen him. But the King, so soon as the son of Harpagus was come into the house, took him and slew him, and cut him limb from limb; and of the flesh he roasted some, and some he boiled; and so, having dressed it with much care, made it 30 ready against the dinner.

35. And when the hour of dinner was come, Harpagus and the other guests sat down to meat; and before Harpagus was set a dish of the flesh of his own son,

wherein was every part, save only the head and the tips of the hands and of the feet.  For these lay apart by themselves with a covering over them.  And when Harpagus had eaten enough, the King asked him, " Was this dish to thy mind?"  And when the man answered 5 that it was indeed to his mind, certain men who had had commandment to do this thing brought the head and the hands and the feet, covered with their cover.

36. These stood before Harpagus, and bad him uncover and take what he would.  And when Harpagus 10 so did, he saw what remained of his son.  Yet, seeing it, he was not amazed, but still commanded himself.  Then the King inquired of him, " Knowest thou what beast this is, of whom thou hast eaten?"  And Harpagus made answer, " I know it; and all that the King doeth 15 is well."  Then he took what was left of the flesh and carried it with him to his house, and buried it.

## CHAPTER VI.

### CYRUS OVERTHROWETH ASTYAGES AND TAKETH THE KINGDOM TO HIMSELF.

1. WHEN King Astyages had punished Harpagus for his transgression in this fashion, he took counsel what he should do with Cyrus.  Wherefore he sent for the 20 same Magians who had interpreted to him his dream concerning his daughter.  And when they were come,

21. **Magians:** These are the Magi, the priests and learned men among the Medes and Persians, the "wise men of the East." *Magic* was originally the art or science of the *Magi*, and a *magician* was a *Magian*.

Astyages inquired of them · how they interpreted the dream.  And they spake again after the former fashion, saying that it was signified by this dream that the boy must needs be a king, if he should live to be of full age.

5  ·2.  And when they had so spoken the King spake thus to them, "The child is yet alive; and it came to pass that in the village wherein he liveth the lads his companions made him their king.  And being so made, he did all things that they who are verily kings are 10 wont to do; for he made some body-guards, and some porters, and some bearers of messages; and to others he gave other offices.  Think ye that this hath aught to do with our matter?"

3.  The Magians said, "If the child is yet alive and 15 was made king after this fashion, but not of any set purpose of thine, thou mayest be of good courage; for he will not be a king again.  And indeed it happeneth oftentimes that oracles and dreams and the like have their fulfillment after this manner in little things, and 20 so come to nothing."

4.  To this Astyages made answer again, "I, too, O Magians, am myself also greatly inclined to this opinion of the matter, that the dream was fulfilled when the boy was called by the name of a king, and that there is 25 no cause why I should fear him any more.  Nevertheless consider the matter well, and advise me how I shall best order these things both for my own house and also for you."  ·

5.  Then the Magians said again, "O King, it is not 30 thy gain only but ours also that thy kingdom should be established.  For verily if it go to this boy, it will pass away from our nation, seeing he is a Persian; and if it so pass, then shall we be as strangers, and shall be of no

account in comparison of the Persians.   But if thou art established in thy kingdom, seeing that thou art of the same country, then shall it in some sort be ours; and we also shall receive great honors at thy hands.   Wherefore we should by all means take thought for thee and 5 for thy dominion.   And now, if we perceived beforehand any peril, surely we should not hide it from thee; but seeing that the dream which made thee afraid hath ended in nothing, we are ourselves of good courage, and would bid thee also be of the same.   As for this boy, 10 send him away out of thy sight to the land of the Persians, even to his father and his mother."

6. When Astyages heard this, he rejoiced exceedingly, and when he had called Cyrus to him he said, " My son, I sought to do thee wrong by reason of a dream that I 15 had, which dream hath failed of its accomplishment; and now seeing that thy good luck hath saved thee, go thy way in peace to the Persians, and I will send some to take thee on thy way.   There wilt thou find thy father and thy mother; and these not such as are the 20 herdsman and his wife."

7. Then Astyages sent away Cyrus to Persia, to his father and mother, who received him with great joy, for they had thought that he was dead.   And when he grew to manhood, there could not be found among his 25 fellows that were of like age one that had such courage and virtue, and was in such favor with all men.

8. Then, after a while, there came to him messengers with gifts from Harpagus; for the man desired exceedingly to have vengeance upon Astyages, but knew not 30 how, being but a private man, he could gain his end; seeing therefore that Cyrus was grown to such excellence, he sought to make friendship and alliance with

the young man; for he judged that they had suffered
wrong, both of them, at the hands of the King.

9. And indeed he had before this wrought for the
same end.   For Astyages was wont to deal cruelly with
5 his people, and Harpagus had talked with certain of the
chief men of the Medes, persuading them that they
should rebel against Astyages and make Cyrus king in
his stead.

10. Now, therefore, all things being ready, he sought
10 to have communication with Cyrus and show him his
purpose, but knew not how he should do it, seeing that
the roads were guarded.   But at the last he devised this
device.   He took a hare, and ripped up the beast, but
took not from it the skin, and having written on a roll
15 all that he would say to Cyrus, put the roll within and
sewed up again the belly of the beast.

11. Then he equipped one of his household, that he
judged to be the most faithful, as for hunting, giving
him nets and the like, and with them the hare.   This
20 man, therefore, he sent into the land of Persia, and
instructed him by word of mouth that he should give
the hare into the hands of Cyrus, and should bid him
open it himself when no man should be near.   All this
was done as he would have it; and Cyrus, having
25 received the hare, opened it with his own hand, and
having found the roll, read it.

12. Now Harpagus had written in the roll these
words: "Son of Cambyses, seeing that the Gods have a
care for thee, for else thou hadst not come to such pros-
30 perity, bethink thee how thou mayest have vengeance
on Astyages, who would have slain thee.   For indeed,
as regards him, thou hadst died long ago, but yet
through the favor of the Gods and my help thou livest.

For I judge that thou hast now for a long time known the truth about thyself, and what I have suffered at the hands of Astyages, because I slew thee not, but rather gave thee to the herdsman. Now, therefore, if thou wilt hearken to me, thou shalt be master of all the 5 country which King Astyages now hath. Persuade the Persians that they revolt, and make war against the Medes.

13. "And it shall happen as thou wouldst have it, whether I be set by Astyages to command the army that 10 shall be sent against thee, or whether any other of the principal men among the Medes be so set. For they will be the first to rebel against him, and will do what they can to the end that they may overthrow Astyages. All things therefore are ready. Only whatever thou 15 doest thou shouldest do quickly."

14. When Cyrus had read these words he took counsel with himself how he might best cause the Persians to revolt. And having considered the matter, he did thus. He wrote in a roll what things he would; and then, 20 having called an assembly of the Persians, opened the roll before them all, and read from it that Astyages had made him commander of the Persians.

15. And when he had read these words he said, "Hearken now, ye Persians; come on the morrow, each 25 man with a reaping-hook." And on the morrow when they came, each man with his reaping-hook, to a certain place in the land of Persia which was covered with thorns and briers, he said to them, "Clear ye me this place of these thorns by sunset," and the place was of 30 eighteen or, it may be, twenty furlongs each way. So the Persians cleared the place as they had been commanded.

16. Then Cyrus said to them, " Come again to me to-morrow, but come ready for a feast;" and he prepared a great feast for the whole army of the Persians, with flesh of goats, and sheep, and oxen, and good store of
5 wine, and all manner of victual, the best that could be provided. And when the Persians were come on the morrow, he made them sit down in a meadow that he had, and feasted them there.

17. And when their meal was ended, Cyrus asked
10 them, saying, " Tell me, on which day did ye fare the better, yesterday or to-day ?" And they answered, " We cannot compare the two, for yesterday we had toil and trouble, but to-day all good things."

18. Then did Cyrus unfold to them his whole counsel,
15 saying, " Men of Persia, the matter stands thus. If ye will hearken to me ye shall have all these good things and others also without number, and that without any need of toiling as slaves. But if ye will not hearken, ye shall have labors without end, such as ye had yester-
20 day. Hearken therefore to me, and be free. For I am sure that I was born by the will of the Gods to bring these things to pass; and as for you, I hold that you are in no wise worse than the Medes, whether as regards valor in battle or as regards other things. I
25 bid you, therefore, rebel this day against King Asty-ages."

19. Cyrus spake these words, and the Persians heark-ened unto him right willingly, taking him for their leader, for they had long since borne it ill that they
30 should be servants to the Medes. And when Astyages heard of these things he sent a messenger to Cyrus commanding him that he should come to him. But

Cyrus said to the man, "Say to Astyages, 'Cyrus will come to thee sooner than thou wouldest have him.'"

20. When Astyages heard these words, he gathered together all the host of the Medes, and made Harpagus captain of the host, forgetting all the wrong that he had done to him, for it was as if the Gods had smitten him with madness.  Now it came to pass that when the battle was joined, some of the Medes fought with all their might against the Persians, knowing nothing of the counsels of Harpagus, and some deserted to the Persians, but the greater part turned their backs and fled.

21. But Astyages, when he knew that the host had fled before the Persians in shameful fashion, yet lost not hope, but sent to Cyrus, threatening him and saying, "Thou shalt not go unpunished."  Then he gathered together all the Medes that were left in the city, both the old men and the lads, and led them out against the Persians and fought with them.  But the Medes fled a second time before the Persians, and Astyages was taken captive.

22. And when he was brought into the camp, Harpagus stood before him, rejoicing over him and reviling him, saying, "See now, thou didst give me the flesh of my son for meat, and lo! thou hast gained for thyself slavery in the place of a kingdom."  Then Astyages looked upon him and said, "Sayest thou then that this deed of Cyrus is of thy doing?"  "Yea," said Harpagus, "for I devised the thing for him, and rightly claim it for my own."

23. Then Astyages made answer, "Surely then thou art more foolish and wicked than all other men.  More foolish art thou, for if thou hast done this thing of thy-

self and so mightest have made thyself a King, why didst thou suffer the power to go to another? And more wicked, seeing that thou hast brought all the nation of the Medes into slavery, bearing anger against 5 me for the little matter of a feast.

24. "For if thou must needs give the kingdom to another rather than keep it for thyself, yet surely thou hadst done well to give it to a Mede rather than to a Persian. But now thou hast brought it about that the 10 Medes, though they were innocent in this matter, having been masters aforetime, are now servants, and that the Persians, having been before our servants, are now our masters."

25. Thus was Astyages driven from his kingdom, 15 having reigned thirty and five years, and by reason of his tyranny having brought great loss to the whole nation of the Medes. Howbeit he suffered nothing at the hands of Cyrus, but lived in peace till the day of his death.

20 26. Of the Persians, of their customs and manner of life, there are some things worthy to be told. They have no images of the Gods, nor temples, nor altars, charging with folly them that use such things, for they hold that the Gods have not the form of men. Their 25 custom is to go up to the tops of the highest mountains that they know, and there do sacrifice to Zeus; but by Zeus is signified the whole circle of the heavens.

27. Also they do sacrifice to the sun, and to the moon, and to the earth, and to fire, and to water, and to 30 the winds. And when they do sacrifice, it is not lawful for any man to pray for good things for himself only, but he prays for them for the whole nation of the Per-

sians, and for the King, remembering that he is one of the Persians, and that so he prayeth for himself.

28. They take great account of birthdays, every man making a feast, according to his means, on his own day. When they have great matters in hand they deliberate 5 upon them, first drinking themselves drunk. But on the morrow, the master of the house where they are layeth before them, being then sober, that which they have resolved, and if it still please them, then it is confirmed. And all things on which they have deliberated 10 being sober, they consider again when they are drunk.

29. Their children they teach three things only, beginning when they are five years old and continuing until twenty years; and the things are these—to ride on horseback, and to shoot with the bow, and to speak 15 the truth.

30. They hold that the most shameful thing that a man can do is to lie; and next to this that he should owe money to another; for they say that the man that oweth money to another cannot choose but lie.    20

---

4. On such days it was customary to have an ox or other large animal baked and served up whole. It is still a common custom in the East to roast sheep whole, even for an ordinary repast, and in Europe the *barbecue* is still popular on public holiday occasions.

11. Tacitus tells us that this method of deliberation was also common among the early Germans, and seems to regard it as a good method of obtaining a well-balanced decision. The passion for wine drinking is as marked among the Persians of the present day, in spite of the prohibitions of the Prophet, as it was in the time of Herodotus.

16. This high regard for truth among the Persians is proved in a remarkable manner by the inscriptions of Darius, in which *lying* is taken as the representative of all evil. When a certain usurpation of the government occurred, it is recorded that "then the *lie* became abounding in the land," and this was regarded as the chief calamity of the usurpation.

## CHAPTER VII.

### THE CITY OF BABYLON. CYRUS TAKETH IT.

1. WHEN Cyrus had overthrown the kingdom of the Lydians, and had conquered also such countries and cities as had appertained thereto, he made war in the next place against the Assyrians. Now the Assyrians
5 have many other great and famous cities, but the greatest and most famous of all is BABYLON, for there, when Nineveh was destroyed, was set up the palace of the King.

2. The city of Babylon is built foursquare, and the
10 measure of each side is one hundred and twenty furlongs. Round about the walls there is a ditch, very deep and broad and full of water; and after the ditch there is a wall, of which the breadth is seventy and five feet, and the height three hundred feet. On the top
15 of the wall, at the sides thereof, are built houses of one story, being so much apart that a chariot with four horses may turn in the space. And in the wall there are a hundred gates, of brass all of them, with posts and lintels of the same.

20 3. The city is divided into two parts, between which floweth the river. Now the name of this river is Euphrates, and it cometh out of the land of Armenia, and floweth into the Red Sea.

4. On either side the wall is pushed forward into the
25 river; also along each bank of the river there runneth a wall of baked brick. The city is built with houses of

---

23. **Red Sea :** A name often given to the Indian Ocean (Erythræan Sea), as well as to its arms, the Persian Gulf and Red Sea.

three stories or four, these being ordered in straight streets that cross each other.   And wheresoever a street goeth down to the river there are gates of brass in the walls of brick that is by the riverside, gates for each street.   Also over and above the outer wall of the city there is an inner wall, of well-nigh equal strength, but in thickness not so great.

5. In each part of the city there was a great building, of which one was the King's palace and the other the temple of Belus.   This temple hath brazen gates, and is foursquare, being two furlongs every way.   In the midst there is a tower which is solid throughout and of the bigness of a furlong each way; and on this tower is built another tower, and yet another upon this, and so forth, seven in all.   Round about these towers are built stairs; and for one who hath climbed halfway a landing-place and chairs where he may rest; and in the topmost tower there is a temple very splendidly furnished, and a couch and a table thereby, but no image.

6. There is another temple below, and in it a statue of Zeus sitting, and before it a table of gold; the throne and the steps are also of gold; and the weight of all is eight hundred talents.   Outside is a golden altar, on which a thousand talents of frankincense were wont to be burnt at the great feast.   Here also was a great statue of gold, twelve cubits high, and solid throughout. This statue Darius was minded to take, but dared not; yet did Xerxes take it, and slew the priest that would have hindered him.

---

10. **Belus** (be'lus): The Greek name of the traditional founder of Babylon, that is, "the dwelling-place of *Bel.*"   From this name came *Baal*, the name of the Phœnician divinity.   *Bel* was the national divinity of the Assyrians, as *Zeus* was of the Greeks.   As the Eastern nations came into closer contact with each other through wars and conquests, one would often adopt the divinities of another.   See *Isaiah*, xlvi. 1; *Jerem.* l. 2.

7. Of this city of Babylon there have been many kings, and two queens. Of these queens the first made for the river great banks, for before her day it used to overflow all the plain of Babylon. The name of this 5 Queen was Semiramis, and the name of the second Queen was Nitocris. This Nitocris, seeing that the kingdom of the Medes increased daily, and that they were not content with what they had, but sought to subdue others, and had conquered many cities, among 10 which was Nineveh, devised a defense against them. For first she caused that the river Euphrates, which before had flowed in a straight course, should now fetch a compass; and this she did by making for it new channels.

15   8. And now one that saileth on this river cometh thrice in three days to the self-same village, and the name of this village is Ardericca. Also she made a great lake, digging it out by the side of the river; and the circuit of this lake is four hundred and twenty fur- 20 longs. Now both these things she did for the same end, that the stream of the river might be the slower and the voyage to Babylon a voyage of many windings, and that when the voyage on the river should be ended, then there should be the voyage on the lake.

25   9. All this was done on that side of the city which

---

1. Babylon revolted against Darius and was besieged and taken by him. Another revolt was put down by Xerxes (zerks'eez), the son of Darius, after his disastrous invasion of Greece. The story of Darius is given in Chaps. XV.–XVII. of Prof. Church's book.

5. Semiramis (se-mǐr'a-mis): This famous queen, it is said, was exposed when a child, like the child Cyrus, and was miraculously fed by doves until she was discovered by a shepherd called Simmas, by whom she was brought up, and from whom she received the name Semiramis. She was celebrated for her surpassing beauty and many heroic achievements. She built the city of Babylon, it was believed, and many wonderful buildings besides, as well as the Hanging Gardens, of which such marvelous tales have been told. See Ragozin's " Story of Assyria."

6. Nitocris (nĭ-to'krĭs): This queen was the mother of Belshazzar, called by the Greeks Labynetus.

looketh toward the country of the Medes; for she would not that the Medes should come into her dominion and learn her affairs.    Also she did this great work for the city.    There being two parts, and the river flowing between them, the citizens had been wont in 5 days of former kings to cross, if they had need, from the one part to the other in boats; and this was a toil to them.    She caused her servants to cut very large stones, and when these were finished, she commanded that they should turn the river into the lake which she 10 had dug.

10. And while this was a-filling, the old stream being now dry, she embanked with brick the side of the river, and the ways also that led thereto from the gates.    But in the middle part of the city she built a bridge with 15 the stones which she had caused to be cut, binding them together with iron and lead.    On this bridge there were laid, so long as it was day, four-cornered timbers, on the which the men of Babylon crossed the bridge.    But at nightfall the timbers were taken away, so that the 20 people of the city might not steal from each other. And when this was finished she brought the river again into his channel.

11. This queen devised this deceit.    She made for herself a tomb over that one of the gates by which the 25 people were chiefly wont to go forth.    On this tomb she wrote certain words of which the significance was this: "IF ONE OF THE KINGS AFTER ME LACK MONEY, LET HIM OPEN THIS TOMB AND TAKE WHAT HE WILL. BUT LET HIM NOT OPEN IT UNLESS HE NEED, FOR IT 30 WILL BE THE WORSE FOR HIM."    This tomb no man would meddle with till Darius came to the kingdom.

12. Now it seemed a grievous thing to Darius that

no man should use the gate, and that money should be
there, and that it should call men to take it, yet should
not be taken.   For no one used the gate because there
was a dead body above his head as he went out.   Where-
5 fore he opened the tomb; but having opened it, found
no money therein, but only the dead body of the queen
and these words, saying, "IF THOU WERE NOT INSATI-
ATE OF MONEY AND A LOVER OF GAIN, THOU HADST
NOT OPENED THE RESTING-PLACE OF THE DEAD."

10    13. Now the king against whom Cyrus made war was
the son of this woman, and his name was Labynetus; and
this had been the name of his father also.   Now when
the Great King, the King of the Persians, marcheth
anywhither he is well provided with food and cattle, and
15 also with water from the river Choaspes, which floweth
by the city of Susa; for the King drinketh not of any
other river save this only.   And many four-wheeled
wagons, drawn by mules, follow the army whithersoever
it goeth, bearing vessels of silver wherein is the water,
20 having been first boiled.

14. But when Cyrus came in his march to the river
Gyndes (this river floweth into the Tigris) there befell
this thing.   While he was seeking to cross the river,
which is of such bigness that ships can sail thereon, one
25 of the white horses which are sacred would have crossed
the river by swimming, and in so doing was drowned.
Then Cyrus was very wroth with the river that had done
him this wrong; and sware that he would make it so

16. **Susa** : One of the Persian capitals, called in the Bible *Shushan.* It was
a vast city, fifteen or twenty miles in circuit.   Alexander found great treasures here.   Its site is now marked only by mounds ; these were opened in
1885 and interesting relics found, which are now in the Louvre Museum in
Paris.
22. **Gyndes** (jin'deez): This is probably the modern *Diyáhah,* although
some think it the *Gangír,* which is actually divided into a multitude of small
streams, at a place called Mendalli.

weak that a woman should be able to cross it without wetting her knee.

15. When he had sworn this oath he divided his army into two parts, and commanded each part that it should dig long trenches by the side of the river—one part working on each side—and the number of the trenches should be one hundred and eighty for each part. And as there was a great multitude of men the work was accomplished in no great space of time; nevertheless they consumed the whole summer in this work.    10

16. So the river Gyndes was made to flow into these trenches, three hundred and sixty in all. And when this was done, and the winter was over, together with the next spring Cyrus led his army to Babylon. And when he came near to the city, the Babylonians came 15 forth to meet him; and when the battle was joined, the Babylonians fled before Cyrus, and were shut up in their city.

17. Now they had gathered provisions for many years, for they knew that Cyrus was a man of war, and sought 20 to conquer all the nations round about. So, therefore, their walls also being very strong, they took no account of the siege; but Cyrus was much troubled, for even after a long time he had done nothing in the matter of taking the city. And whether he himself devised the 25 device, or another devised it for him, cannot be said; but this he did. He divided his army into two portions; and of these he set one above the city where the river floweth into it, and the other he set below it where the river floweth out.    30

18. To these he gave commandment that when they should see the river so shallow that a man could cross it they should enter the city by it. And when he had

thus ordered things, he himself departed with such of
the army as were of no account for war, and when he
came to the lake which Nitocris, Queen of Babylon,
had made by the riverside, then did he thus.   He made
5 a great trench, and turned the river into the lake, which
in those days was a marsh only and not filled with
water.

19. And when this had been done the river became
shallow, so that a man might cross it, and the Persians

BABYLONIAN CAPTIVES.

10 to whom the commandment had been given, perceiving
what had happened, and that the water now came but
up to the middle of a man's thigh, entered the city of
Babylon by way of the river.

20. Now if the men of Babylon had known before-
15 hand or perceived the thing that Cyrus was doing, then
all these Persians had perished miserably, for they would
have shut all the gates leading down to the river, and
would have gone up themselves on to the walls that were
built along the banks of the river, and so would have

had the Persians as it were in a fish-trap.    But in truth the Persians came upon them unawares.

21. Now the bigness of the city was such that they who dwelt in the middle parts knew not that the outside parts had been taken; but played and danced and de- 5 lighted themselves, till indeed they were made to know it in such fashion as they liked not.

22. This land of Babylon is a very good land.    For while all the rest of Asia nourisheth the Great King and his army for eight months, this alone nourisheth 10 him for four months.    And there cometh to him that holdeth this province under the King a measure of silver containing twelve gallons day by day.    Rain falleth not often, but the plain is watered by the river, as is also the land of Egypt; and it beareth wheat as doth no 15 other country in the whole earth, even two hundredfold, and, when the harvest is of the best, three hundredfold.

23. They have this law about marriage.    In every village and town they gather together such maidens as are of a marriageable age into one place, the multitude 20 of men standing in a circle round about them.    Then there standeth up a herald in the midst and selleth

---

7. The Jews were at this time held in bondage at Babylon and gave Cyrus valuable assistance.  For this he gave them their liberty, sent them back to Jerusalem, aided them in rebuilding the Temple, and restored to them all the sacred gold and silver vessels which Nebuchadnezzar had brought to Babylon.  For the Biblical account, see the book of *Daniel*, v., *Ezra*, i.-vi., *II Chronicles*, xxxvi. 22, 23.  This conquest of Cyrus was foretold in the prophecy of *Isaiah*, xiv. 1.  See also *Isaiah*, xlvi., xlvii.

14. Says Herodotus: "The river does not, as in Egypt, overflow the corn-lands of its own accord, but is spread over them by the hand, or by the help of engines.  The whole of Babylonia is, like Egypt, intersected with canals." The modern method of irrigation is to draw the water from the river to the top of the bank by means of oxen and ropes passed over a roller between two upright posts.

17. Herodotus adds: "The blade of the wheat-plant and barley-plant is often four fingers in breadth.  As for the millet and the sesame, I shall not say to what height they grow, though within my own knowledge; for I am not ignorant that what I have already written concerning the fruitfulness of Babylonia must seem incredible to those who have never visited the country."

them, one by one; and the manner of selling them is
this.    First he taketh her that is counted the fairest in
the whole company, and when she has been sold for a
great sum of money, then her that is the next in fair-
5 ness.

24. Then all the wealthy men among the Babylonians, being minded to marry, contend with each other
who shall buy those that excel in beauty; but such of
the common folk as are minded to marry care not at all
10 for beauty, but take the maidens that are less comely to
look upon, and money with them.

25. For when the herald had finished his selling of
the beautiful maidens, then he taketh her that is worst
favored in the company, or, it may be, maimed of a
15 limb, and offereth her.    And the men say for how much
money they will take her to wife; and to him that say-
eth the least is she given.    And the gold that the rich
men pay for the well-favored among the maidens, this
do the poor men receive with the ill-favored.    Nor is it
20 lawful for a man to give his daughter in marriage to
any that he will.

26. Another excellent custom have they with them
that are sick.    These they carry forth from their houses
into the market-place; for they have no physicians in
25 their country.    Then all that come near give their
counsel about the sick man, if any one hath himself endured such disease as the sick man hath, or hath seen
any other enduring it.    And they tell each of them in
their turn how they were cured of such disease, or may

_____

22. Herodotus seems to regard this custom as universal, but discoveries
in recent years have shown that it was not so.    There is an interesting
account of Babylonian customs in Ragozin's "Story of Media, Babylon,
and Persia" (pp. 244–260), taken from tablets discovered in 1874, which are
believed to be the private account-books of a family of Jewish money-
lenders.

have seen others cured.   But it is not lawful for any to pass by the sick man till he shall have made inquiry what his disease may be.

---

## CHAPTER VIII.

### CYRUS MAKETH WAR AGAINST THE MASSAGETÆ, AND DIETH.

1. WHEN Cyrus had conquered the Babylonians and taken their city, it came into his heart to make war 5 against the Massagetæ and to subdue them.   This is a very great and valiant nation, dwelling toward the sun-rising, beyond the river Araxes.   This Araxes is a great river, having in it islands that are of the bigness of Lesbos.   In these islands, which are, they say, many in 10 number, there dwell men who eat in the summer all manner of roots, but for the winter they store up such fruits as they have found to be good for food.

2. They have among them one tree that beareth fruits of a very wonderful kind.   The men assemble in 15 companies and light a fire, and sit round the fire in a circle; then they throw upon this fire of the fruit of the tree; and when they smell the savor of the fruit that is thrown upon the fire, they grow drunken with the smell thereof, even as the Greeks grow drunken with 20 wine; and more fruit being thrown upon the fire they grow yet more drunken, till at the last they come to

---

6. **Massagetæ** (mas-saj'e-te): A wild and warlike Scythian people, dwelling near the Caspian Sea.   The Araxes River is the same as the Jaxartes.

dancing and singing.   In the marshes of this river where
it floweth into the sea—and it floweth, they say, through
forty mouths—there dwell men that have fish only for
food, eating them raw, and for clothing they have the
5 skins of seals.

3. Now the cause wherefore Cyrus had it in his mind
to make war against the Massagetæ was this: that his
spirit was puffed up and exalted with many things, as
with his birth, from which he judged that he was
10 above the measure of a man, and with his good luck
that had followed him in his wars; for of all the nations
against whom he had been minded to make war not one
had been able to escape.   Now the ruler of the Massagetæ in those days was a woman, whose husband was
15 dead, and the name of this woman was Tomyris.

4. Cyrus therefore sent messengers to her, saying that
he would fain take her to wife.   But Tomyris, knowing
that he wished not for her but for the kingdom of the
Massagetæ, denied herself to him.   Then Cyrus, when
20 he could not prevail by craft, marched to the river
Araxes, and made war openly against the Massagetæ,
for he began to make bridges of ships over the river by
which his army might be able to cross, and to build also
towers for defense upon the ships.

25    5. But while he was busying himself with these
things, Queen Tomyris sent to him, saying, "O King of
the Medes, cease from doing these things that thou art
doing; for thou canst not know whether they will be to
thy profit.   Cease from them therefore, and rule thy
30 own people, and be content also to see me ruling over
my people.   Yet, as I know that thou wilt not follow
this my counsel, and that there is nothing that is less to
thy mind than to be at peace, I offer thee this.   If

thou greatly desirest to make trial of the strength of the Massagetæ, then cease from this thy labor of making bridges across the Araxes, and when we have gone back three days' march from the river, then take thy army across; or, if thou wouldst rather have it so, do thou on thy part go back three days' journey from the river, and abide our coming."

6. When Cyrus heard this, he called together the chief men of the Persians, and laid the whole matter before them, inquiring of them which of these two things he should rather do. For the most part the council of the Persians agreed together that he should suffer Tomyris and her army to enter his country. But Crœsus the Lydian, being present in the council, agreed not with this opinion, but gave contrary advice, saying, "I have said to thee aforetime, O King, that from the day when Zeus made thee lord over me, I cease not to turn away, if it may be, any evil that I may perceive coming upon thy house. And, indeed, my own troubles have been hard teachers to me.

7. "Now, therefore, if thou countest thyself to be immortal and the army which thou rulest to be immortal also, there shall be no need that I should show forth my opinion. But if thou knowest thyself to be a man only, and thine army to be of men only, then consider that there is as it were a wheel of the fortunes of men, and that this wheel turneth round always, and suffereth not the same man to be always in prosperity. Now, my opinion is contrary to the opinion of these.

8. "If thou sufferest these men to come into thy

---

26. Among the Greeks and Romans there was a goddess of fortune, called Fortuna, who was usually represented with a wheel, the token of instability.

country, there is this peril. If thou fleest before them, then thou losest thy whole kingdom. But if, on the contrary, thou comest into their country and they flee before thee, then thou wilt conquer them altogether. 5 Also, it doth not become thee, being such an one as Cyrus the son of Cambyses, to give place before a woman. But hearken now unto me, and I will tell thee what thou shalt do.

9. "These Massagetæ have no knowledge of the good 10 things of the Persians. Do thou, therefore, kill for these men great store of sheep, and cause their flesh to be cooked, and furnish a feast for them in our camp. Forget not also to fill bowls with wine without stint, and to set out all manner of good things. Which when 15 thou hast done, leave there in the camp that which is of least account in thy army, and go back again with that which remains to the river. For I am persuaded that these men, when they see these good things, will fly forthwith upon them, and that we shall find occasion to 20 do great things against them."

10. Then Cyrus rejected the former counsel, and chose the counsel of Crœsus. Wherefore he sent a message to Queen Tomyris, that she should depart from the river, for that he was resolved to cross over into her 25 country. After this he called his son Cambyses, to whom also he had left the kingdom after him, and committed Crœsus into his hands, bidding him deal kindly with him and honor him, if he should not prosper in battle with the Massagetæ. And when he had sent 30 these two away into the land of Persia, he himself crossed the river Araxes with his army.

11. In the night after he had crossed the river he saw a vision in his sleep, and the vision was this. He saw

the eldest of the sons of Hystaspes, having wings upon his shoulders, with one whereof he shadowed the whole land of Asia, and with the other the whole land of Europe. Now, the eldest of the sons of Hystaspes, who was of the house of Achæmenes, was Darius, being then about 5 twenty years of age; and he had been left in the land of Persia as not being of age to go with the host.

12. And Cyrus, when he woke from sleep, considered with himself what this vision might mean; and because it seemed to him a very great matter, he called Hystas- 10 pes, and taking him apart by himself, said to him, "Hystaspes, thy son is manifestly proved to be laying plots against me and my kingdom. And how I know this thing thou shalt hear. The Gods have great care for me, and show me beforehand all things that shall 15 come to pass. Now, therefore, in this night past I saw a vision in my sleep—even the eldest of thy sons with wings upon his shoulders, with one whereof he shadowed the land of Asia, and with the other the land of Europe. 20

13. "Seeing then that I have had this vision, it must needs be that he is laying plots against me. Do thou, therefore, depart with all speed into the land of Persia, and see that, when I shall have subdued this country and am returned, he shall be brought to the trial." This 25 said Cyrus thinking that Darius was laying plots against him. But in very truth the Gods showed him by this vision that he should die in that land, and that his kingdom should be given to Darius.

14. Then Hystaspes made answer, "My lord the 30

---

5. **Achæmenes** (a-keem'e-neez): The ancestor of the Persian kings, whose descendants were called *Achœmenidœ.* Hystaspes (his-tas'peez) was thus of the royal house.

King, the Gods forbid that there should be any Persian
who would plot against thee, and if such there be, may
he be brought to naught.   For thou hast made the Persians free who were slaves before, and to be the rulers
5 of all men in place of being ruled by others.   If, therefore, it be signified by this vision that my son is plot-
ting against thee, be sure that I will deliver him to thee
to do with him as thou wilt."

15. When Hystaspes had said this, he crossed the
10 Araxes and went his way into the land of Persia, that
he might keep Darius his son against King Cyrus
should return.   And when Cyrus had gone a day's
march from the river Araxes, he did according to the
word of Crœsus.   For he returned with the better part
15 of his army to the river and left the worse part behind.

16. Then there came a third part of the army of the
Massagetæ, and fought with those that Cyrus had left
behind, and slew them.   And when they had vanquished their enemies, seeing the feast that had been
20 prepared, they sat down and feasted ; and having filled
themselves with food and wine, they lay down to sleep.
But while they slept the Persians came upon them, and
slew many of them, and took yet more of them alive.
And among them that they took was the captain of the
25 host of the Massagetæ, being a son of Queen Tomyris,
whose name was Spargapises.

17. And when the queen knew what had befallen the
army and her son also, she sent unto Cyrus, saying,
" Be not puffed up, O Cyrus, thou that never canst be
30 satisfied with blood, by reason of this thing that thou
hast done.   For thou hast taken of the fruit of the
vine, with which ye are wont to fill yourselves to madness, so that when the wine enters into you, there come

forth from you all manner of evil words ; this, I say, thou hast taken, and with it hast prevailed over my son, vanquishing him by craft, and not by strength.

18. " Now, therefore, I give thee this counsel. Give back to me my son, and go thy way out of this land un- 5 hurt, having worked thy will upon the third part of the army of the Massagetæ. But if thou wilt not do according to my words, then I swear by the Sun, who is the lord of the Massagetæ, that though thou canst not be satisfied with blood, yet will I satisfy thee."    10

19. But Cyrus, when this message was brought to him, took no heed of it. After this, Spargapises, the son of Queen Tomyris, when the wine had left him, and he knew into what trouble he had come, made entreaty to Cyrus that he might be loosened awhile from his 15 bonds. But so soon as ever he was loosed, he slew himself.

20. After this Queen Tomyris, seeing that Cyrus would not listen to her counsel, gathered together all her army, and joined battle with the Persians. And of 20 all battles that have ever been fought among barbarians was never one fiercer than this battle. First they stood apart and shot at each other with bows ; and when their arrows were spent, they fell upon each other with spears and swords, and so fought.    25

21. For a long time they contended against each other, and neither the one nor the other would give place. But at the last the Massagetæ prevailed over the Persians. And the greater part of the army of the Persians perished on that day, and Cyrus himself also 30 was slain, having reigned twenty and eight years. Then Queen Tomyris, having first filled a skin with man's blood, commanded ;hat they should search among the

dead bodies for the body of Cyrus.    And when they had found it, she cut off his head and thrust it into the skin, and scoffed at the dead body, saying, " Thou didst take my son by craft when I could have prevailed over 5 thee in battle ;  and now, as I sware, I will satisfy thee with blood."

22. Thus Cyrus the son of Cambyses the Persian died in the land of the Massagetæ, and Cambyses his son reigned in his stead.

---

7. It is believed that the tomb of Cyrus still exists at *Murg-Aub*, the ancient *Pasargadæ*.   On a square base, composed of immense blocks of beautiful white marble, rising in steps, stands a chamber or house-like structure, with sloping roof, which once probably contained a sarcophagus' The natives call it the tomb of the Mother of Solomon.

# PRONOUNCING VOCABULARY.

NOTE: Final *a* is sounded as in the word *opera*.

Abæ, a'be.
Abdera, ab de'ra.
Achæmenes, a-keem'e-neez.
Achæmenidæ, ak-e-men'i-de.
Adrastus, a-dras'tus.
Æolia, e-o'lǐ-a.
Agamedes, ag-a-me'deez.
Alcmæon, alk-me'on.
Alyattes, a-lǐ at'teez.
Amasis, a-ma'sis.
Amphiaraus, am-fǐ-a-ra'us.
Anabasis, a-nab'a-sis
Apollo, a-pol'lo.
Araxes, a-raks'eez.
Ardericca, ar-de-rik'ka.
Arganthonius, ar-gan-tho'nǐ-us.
Argos, ar'gos.
Aristodicus, a-ris-to-di'kus.
Armenia, ar-me'nǐ-a.
Artembares, ar-tem'ba-reez.
Artemis, ar'te-mis.
Aryenis, a-rǐ-e'nis.
Asia, a'shǐ-a.
Aspasia, as-pa'zhǐ-a.
Astyages, as-ti'a-jeez.
Atarnes, a-tar'neez.
Athens, ath'enz.
Atropos, at'ro-pos.
Atys, a'tis.

Baal, ba'al.
Babylon, bab'ǐ-lon.
Bacchus, bak'kus.
Belus, be'lus.
Bias, bi'as.
Biton, bi'ton.
Bœotia, be-o'shǐ-a.
Branchidæ, bran'ki de.

Cambyses, kam-bi'seez.
Cappadocia, kap-pa-do'shǐ-a.
Caria, ka'rǐ-a.

Carians, ka'rǐ-anz.
Carthage, kar'thāj.
Chios, ki'os.
Choaspes, ko-as'peez.
Cilicia, sǐ-lish'ǐ-a.
Cleobis, kle'o-bis.
Clotho, klo'tho.
Colchis, kol'kis.
Crœsus, kre'sus.
Cumæ, ku'me.
Cyaxares, si-aks'a-reez.
Cyrnus, sir'nus.
Cyrus, si'rus.

Darius, da-ri'us.
Delphi, del'-fǐ.
Diana, dǐ-a'na.
Dodòna, do-do'na.

Ecbatana, ek-bat'a-na.
Egbatana, eg-bat'a-na.
Egypt, e'jipt.
Eleusis, e-lu'sis.
Endymion, en-dim'ǐ-on.
Ephesian, e-fe'zhǐ-an.
Ephesus, ef'e-sus.
Epirus, e-pi'rus.
Euphrates, u-fra'teez.
Euripides, u-rip'i-deez.

Fates, fāts.
Fortuna, for-tu'na.

Gordias, gor'dǐ-as.
Gygæa, ji-je'a.
Gyndes, jin'deez.

Halicarnassus, hal-i-kar-nas'sus.
Halys, ha'lis.
Hammon, ham'mon.
Harpagus, har'pa-gus.
Here, he're.

93

Herodotus, he-rod'o-tus.
Hesperides, hes-pĕr'i-deez.
Hyrœades, hi-re'a-deez.
Hystaspes, his-tas'peez.

Ionia, i-o'nĭ-a.
Isaiah, i-za'ya.

Juno, ju'no.
Jupiter, ju'pĭ-ter.

Labynetus, lab-i-ne'tus.
Lacedæmon, las-e-de'mon.
Lachesis, lak'e-sis.
Lacrines, lak'ri-neez.
Lesbos, les'bos.
Libya, lib'ĭ-a.
Lybian, lib'ĭ-an.
Lycians, lish'ĭ-anz.
Lydia, lid'ĭ-a.
Lydus, li'dus.

Magians, ma'jĭ-anz.
Mandane, man-da'ne.
Manes, ma'neez.
Mardian, mar'dĭ-an.
Massagetæ, mas-saj'e-te.
Mazares, maz'a-reez.
Medes, meedz.
Meles, me'leez.
Midas, mi'das.
Miletus, mi-le'tus.
Mitradates, mit-ra-da'teez.
Mitylene, mit-i-le'ne.
Mysia, mizh'ĭ-a.

Nebuchadnezzar, neb-u-kad-nez'-zar.
Nineveh, nin'e-vĕ.
Nitocris, ni-to'kris.

Olympus, o-lim'pus.

Pactolus, pak-to'lus.
Pactyas, pak'tĭ-as.
Palestine, pal'es-tīn.
Panyasis, pa-ni'a-sis.
Parcæ, par'se.
Pasargadæ, pa-sar'ga-de.
Pelops, pe'lops.
Pericles, pĕr'i-kleez.
Persians, per'shĭ-anz.
Pharaoh, fa'ro.
Phidias, fid'ĭ-as.
Phocæa, fo-se'a.

Phocis, fo'sis.
Phraortes, fra-or'teez.
Phrygia, frij'ĭ-a.
Pittacus, pit'ta-kus.
Plato, pla'to.
Plutarch, plu'tark.
Priene, pri-e'ne.
Pterium, te'rĭ-um.
Pythermus, pĭ-ther'mus.
Pythia, pith'ĭ-a.

Rhegium, re'jĭ-um.

Samos, sa'mos.
Sandanis, san'da-nis.
Sardis, sar'dis.
Scythia, sĭth'ĭ-a.
Semiramis, se-mĭr'a-mis.
Sinope, sĭ-no'pe.
Smyrna, smer'na.
Solon, so'lon.
Sophocles, sof'o-kleez.
Spaco, spa'ko.
Spargapises, spar-ga-pi'seez.
Sparta, spar'ta.
Susa, su'sa.
Syennesis, si-en'ne-sis.

Tabalus, tab'a-lus.
Tacitus, tas'i-tus.
Tartessus, tar-tes'sus.
Teispes, te-is'peez.
Tellus, tel'lus.
Telmessus, tel-mes'sus.
Thales, tha'leez.
Thrace, thrās.
Thucydides, thu-sid'i-deez.
Thurii, thu'rĭ-i.
Tigris, ti'gris.
Tios, ti'os.
Tomyris, tom'i-ris.
Trophonius, tro-fo'nĭ-us.
Tyre, tīr.
Tyrrhenus, tĭr-re'nus.
Tyrsenia, tĭr-se'nĭ-a.

Umbri, um'brī.

Venus, ve'nus.

Xanthus, zan'thus.
Xenophon, zen'o-fon.
Xerxes, zerks'eez.

Zeno, ze'no.

www.ingramcontent.com/pod-product-compliance
Lightning Source LLC
Chambersburg PA
CBHW020034030726
47499CB00007B/2414